A
BLIND
EYE

A BLIND EYE

a novel by

JULIE DAINES

Covenant Communications, Inc.

Cover image: *Artistic Eye* © Bluberries Advertising

Cover design copyright © 2013 by Covenant Communications, Inc.

Published by Covenant Communications, Inc.
American Fork, Utah

Printed in the United States of America
First Printing: February 2013

19 18 17 16 15 14 13   10 9 8 7 6 5 4 3 2 1

ISBN 978-1-62108-252-1

To my sister

I wish you could be here for this, even though you would have
read the last chapter first and ruined the whole story.

ACKNOWLEDGMENTS

OF THE ONE MILLION PEOPLE I need to thank for their help, support, and expertise on this project, I'll start with my fantastic writers group, The Sharks and Pebbles: Yamile Mendez, Jaime Theler, Taffy Lovell, and Scott Rhoades. Your input has been the difference between life and death—at least for some of the characters. Special thanks to Tiffany Dominquez, who planted the writing seed in the first place, and to Michelle Ratto, beta reader extraordinaire, who wasn't afraid to tell me she liked the other book better.

I'd like to thank Kirk Shaw, whose support and encouragement has meant more to me than he'll ever know, and Samantha Millburn for getting the manuscript into shipshape form, and the whole team at Covenant for all their talent.

The biggest thanks of all goes to my husband, Dave, who would give me the moon if he thought it would encourage me with my writing. The tuna sandwich is for you.

There is none so blind as those who cannot see.

—Old English Proverb

CHAPTER ONE

CHRISTIAN VS. THE STOWAWAY

I ALWAYS THOUGHT MAKING LIFE-or-death decisions would be more dramatic. Thrilling. Like something from a movie. I should have known better.

Last week I chose death. It didn't work out.

Today, after serious reconsideration, I chose life. And for me, that meant leaving.

I tossed the last of my gear into the back of my Range Rover—the car my father gave me just after I turned sixteen. That was over a year ago. He hadn't spoken to me since. Maybe I should have felt guilty for using it to run away, but I didn't. Just because he had a son didn't mean he wanted one.

I drove a few blocks to the 7-Eleven and filled the car up with gas. I bought some ranch-flavored corn nuts and a few bottles of sports drink. Bouquets of wilting roses stood in a rack by the counter. I grabbed a bundle of those too.

In ten minutes, I arrived at my next stop. The cemetery. I pulled in and followed the wide curve of the lane until I came to an immense cedar tree. I took the cellophane-wrapped flowers and wove my way through the forest of headstones to my mother's grave.

I'd sat there many times, telling her about Dad, how he hated me, and how my life was messed. It never changed anything, but I felt better—for a few days at least. She died when I was nine. My dad remarried last year. Enter trophy wife, Gloria. I didn't know if he made her feel the way she did or if it simply came naturally, but I suspected she hated me too.

Eight years was a long time. Most of my memories of Mom were as faint and eroded as the weathered tombstones surrounding me. More than anything, I remembered after she died. When Dad fell apart and never really came back. At least not to me. For him, it was like I didn't exist.

And now, the time had come to make that a reality. How else could I avoid a repeat of last week's lapse in judgment?

"Hey, Mom. I won't be seeing you for a while. I'm heading out." I laid the flowers on her smooth headstone and trudged back to my car.

I took the Sunset Highway heading east and crossed the Willamette River, skirting downtown Portland.

Just as I reached the end of town, something bumped the back of my seat. "What the—"

I craned my neck to look behind me. The driver next to me laid on his horn, and I swerved back into my lane. Another bump and a rustling sound. I'd left my car doors open while I'd loaded my stuff; maybe a stray cat had crawled in.

I pulled off onto the shoulder, jumped out, and opened the back door. Something huddled behind my seat, hidden under the clothes and bags, but it wasn't an animal. It was a girl.

"Get out," I ordered.

Her hands fumbled to grip the handle. Leaning heavily on it, she slowly stepped out.

She was small but definitely older than I first thought. Sixteen, maybe seventeen. She had a layer of chin-length, bright-pink hair framing her face; the rest was short and jet-black. She wore a tight, black T-shirt that had a red circle with a blue line through it and the words *Mind the Gap*.

A meticulously shredded jean miniskirt hung to her thighs, followed by black tights. Heavy, black combat boots with laces *and* buckles completed the look.

I took a step back for a better view. Portland had its share of unique inhabitants, but we tended to err on the side of earthy *save-the-planet*. I was pretty sure we drank recycled toilet water. Maybe she was part of the crowd that hung out under Burnside Bridge. I tipped my head to the side. Not bad-looking though, in an unconventional, punk kind of way.

"Please don't leave me on the motorway," she said in a thick British accent. Dark sunglasses concealed her eyes, and she kept her head down, speaking to my feet.

"Who are you?" When I asked, her head snapped up, and a tiny, diamond nose stud sparkled in the late afternoon sun.

"Scarlett."

That told me nothing, except her parents were terrible at naming. "What are you doing in my car?"

"I needed a lift." Her voice quivered, and she wrung her hands together hard enough to remove a layer of skin.

"Sorry to be the one to tell you this, Scarlett"—when I said her name, I tried to mimic her fancy accent—*Scaahlett*—"but you can't just go around sneaking into people's cars. Not unless you're a carjacker or a rapist." Not that she posed much of a threat. She couldn't weigh more than ninety pounds wet. "Where did you come from?"

"London."

That wasn't exactly what I had asked. I hoped for something more along the lines of how she'd managed to slink into my car undetected.

Whatever. She wasn't my problem. I had a plan, and it did not involve her. Especially after the whole stowaway act. I pointed up the road. "There's an exit about a quarter mile up the highway. Follow it to the airport. You'll find lots of taxis, buses, and airplanes to take you anywhere you want to go. But you know what? I'm not one of them." I climbed into my car, rolled down the window, and waved. "See ya, Scarlett."

By the time I'd pulled away, her shoulders shook and she was wiping her face with both hands. I checked the rearview mirror as I rounded the bend in the highway. She hadn't moved.

I pounded the steering wheel with both hands. "Shoot!" I'd promised myself I wouldn't turn out like him. And now I had turned my back on someone. Just like he had turned his on me. My dad cared nothing about my life. He cared about looking good for the firm and avoiding anything that might remind him that he had a son. When it came to lowlifes like me, he couldn't be bothered.

But that wasn't me.

I could at least give her a ride to the airport. It was the closest hub of transportation. I turned off at the exit I'd told her to walk to, crossed the viaduct, and reentered the highway on the southbound side. It was less than a mile to the next exit. I got off and turned around again, heading back onto the northbound road. Would she still be there? What if a creep had picked her up? My departure strategy had not included a guilt trip.

She was there. She hadn't taken one step. I stopped the car in front of her. A line of shiny tears leaked out from under her sunglasses. I leaned across the shotgun seat and flung the door open.

"Fine," I said. "I'll take you to the airport."

She reached out her hand and stepped forward. She fumbled again for a handhold then pulled herself in.

"Thanks," she said, sniffing.

"Sure." Why do girls do that? Cry. I hate it. They turn on the faucet, and suddenly, we can't help ourselves. We have to fix it. Stupid, stupid girl.

I put the car in drive and merged into the traffic. Five minutes later we pulled up in the passenger pickup lane of Portland International Airport.

She'd probably just gotten separated from her family and didn't know how to get back. "See over there?" I pointed out the passenger window, my arm almost brushing the tip of her nose. "Cross that walkway, and you'll find the taxis, buses, and hotel shuttles."

She stared straight out the front windshield.

"Do you have a hotel?"

"No."

"Is your family here?"

"No."

"Where are they?"

She shrugged. "Dunno. I haven't seen them in ages." She shifted in her seat and tucked a pink strand of hair behind her ear. "I was away, at a special school."

Ah. She rode the short bus. Maybe she just needed money for a cab. I leaned to the side and pried my wallet out of my back pocket then dropped some money in her lap. I had plenty—after stealing a wad from my dad's safe before I hit the road. "This should help you get wherever you need to go."

She took the money and thumbed through it. "How much is it?"

Didn't she just count it? Maybe she struggled with American money. It could be tricky—with the numbers printed in every corner and then spelled out at the bottom . . . on both sides. I rolled my eyes. "It's a hundred dollars."

"Five twenties?"

"Uh, yeah." I was beginning to see why she went to a *special* school. Not everyone home upstairs.

"Thanks." She felt around the door until she found the latch, opening it with a soft click. Her foot dangled out of the car, searching for the ground.

A suspicion crept up inside me. "Scarlett, wait."

She turned her head but didn't quite face me.

I waved my hand in front of her face. No reaction. I stuck my tongue out. She didn't respond. I waved my hand again, harder. Still nothing.

She was blind?

I'd left a blind girl standing on the side of the freeway in the middle of rush-hour traffic. No wonder she'd looked terrified. So much for avoiding the guilt trip. And now I was dumping her on the curb of PDX? I couldn't do it. I was a better person than that. Or at least I wanted to be.

"Where are you headed, exactly?" I asked.

She shrugged. "Where are you headed?"

"Vancouver." I had relatives there that I thought might take me in. From my mom's side, of course. But no way was the little stowaway coming with me.

"Sounds lovely."

I looked at her again. No purse, no bags, apparently no money. "Vancouver, BC. That's in Canada." Vancouver, Washington, was half a mile away across the river. I wanted to make sure she knew which Vancouver I meant.

"Brilliant."

I'd known her a total of ten minutes. Did she actually believe I'd take her with me? Time to put a stop to that line of thinking. "Do you have your passport with you? This isn't the European Union. You have to have ID to cross the borders."

She reached into a pocket and produced a laminated card. It had her picture, her name—Scarlett Becket—and her birth date. She'd just turned seventeen. According to the fine print, this was an ID card for the Shepherd Hill School for the Gifted located in Islington, London N6. No phone number.

I had assumed her *special* school was in Portland. Otherwise, what was she doing here without family or friends?

A knock at my window made me jump. I rolled it down a few inches, and the traffic guy in a bright-yellow vest informed me that this lane was for active loading and unloading only. As if we hadn't been listening to a woman's voice repeating that exact phrase over the loud speakers since we'd pulled up to the curb.

"Sorry," I told him. "We were just leaving."

Scarlett closed her door and smiled at me—or at least in my direction. This chink in my plans irritated me, but I was willing to be the Good Samaritan.

I drove out of the airport and back toward the freeway. Might as well continue north. We were right on the state border, and I wanted to get into Washington before it got too late—just in case my dad turned paternal. I shook my head. I didn't know why I thought that. I could've moved next door, and he wouldn't have come looking. He'd probably be first in line at the post office filing a change of address for me.

I pressed my fingertips to my temple, massaging in circles, and took a deep breath. "Okay. Let's just start over. My name is Christian," I said in the most pleasant voice I could muster. "How about we stop for some dinner and you can tell me what your deal is and where you're supposed to be." I could always double back and drop her off somewhere later.

"Thanks." She turned her head away, like she was looking out her side window. But then she slipped her fingers under the sunglasses and wiped her eyes.

Oh great. Tears again. "Hey," I said. "It's okay. I'm sorry I left you on the side of the road. I was an idiot."

"Yeah," she whispered, her face still turned away.

"I'll help you find whoever you're here with, okay?"

"I'm here alone."

How did she get in the middle of Portland without someone to help her? How does a blind girl from London end up hiding in the back of your car in Oregon? I opened my mouth to ask then changed my mind. It might upset her more. I filed my questions away, saving them for the restaurant.

We crossed the Columbia River, the setting sun reflecting orange off the water. I drove a few minutes into the suburbs of Vancouver—Washington—and then exited the highway. A billboard announced a Shari's coming up. Not my favorite restaurant, but since they specialized in breakfasts, I hoped it would be quiet.

I pulled into a parking space and killed the motor. "How long have you been blind?"

"Since birth." She didn't seem surprised that I'd figured it out. But I had to admit, she'd done a good job keeping it to herself. She could've mentioned that in the beginning and saved us both a lot of hassle. But judging by her Day-Glo hair and less-than-subtle outfit, she didn't want her impairment to be the first thing people noticed.

"Now, tell me again. How did you get here? Alone?"

"I was kidnapped," she whispered.

CHAPTER TWO

CHRISTIAN VS. THE WOMEN'S BATHROOM

I STARED AT SCARLETT, ONE hand frozen on the steering wheel and one on the gear shift. Jaw dangling somewhere in between. "Are you serious?"

"D'you see me laughing?"

Uh, no. Definitely not laughing. Should I ask her about it? If she wanted to talk, wouldn't she tell me on her own? Or was she playing me? She could have made the story up to garner sympathy. I had a very small comfort zone, and at the moment, I was so far out of it, it wasn't even a speck in the distance. She'd finally stopped crying, and I really wanted to keep it that way. "You okay for dinner?"

"Yeah." She opened her car door and slid out, closing it behind her. Then she just stood there under the cloudy evening sky, waiting.

I scanned the parking lot hopefully, but there weren't any spare seeing-eye dogs lounging nearby. I got out and walked around to her. Should I hold her hand? That seemed a little . . . intimate. I reached down and took her wrist.

"Is this okay?" I asked, trying to pretend I didn't feel completely awkward. I'd never guided anyone who couldn't see before. At least, not for real. I'd done those trust exercises in Scouts, where you lead a blindfolded friend around an obstacle course. But we mostly tried to see who could mess up the other person more, leading them into poles and trees or forgetting to mention concrete steps.

She pulled her wrist free and then hooked her hand around the crook of my arm. "It's easier like this." Her head came to my shoulder.

I'd do the dinner thing, figure out where she wanted me to drop her, then *hasta la vista*. We'd go our separate ways.

"Two?" the waitress asked. She was a middle-aged lady and looked pretty fit for her years.

"Yeah. Booth, please," I said.

She nodded and led us through the maze of tables to the booths lining the far wall. Scarlett moved closer to me, the side of her body pressed against my arm. The waitress gestured to a booth, and we settled into our table in the back. The place was practically empty for six o'clock on a Thursday night.

The waitress placed a greasy plastic menu full of color pictures in front of us then asked if we wanted something to drink. I ordered a soda, and Scarlett asked for hot chocolate. It was then I noticed she was shivering. She wore only her short-sleeve *Mind the Gap* T-shirt, and the fall evening was cold.

I shrugged off my jacket and held it out to her. "Here."

After a pause she said, "What?"

Stupid me. I stood up and draped it around her shoulders.

She slipped her arms into the sleeves and pushed them up to expose her hands. She looked even smaller, lost in my big jacket.

I skimmed the menu, trying to decide what I was in the mood for. "Do you know what you're having?" I asked without glancing up, falling back on the standard restaurant question when you needed to make conversation.

"I'll have what you have," she said.

Her menu lay untouched on the table in front of her. This was harder than I thought.

"What do you like? They have a little bit of everything. Pasta, hamburgers, chicken, and sandwiches. Or breakfast stuff, if that's what you want."

"Is it expensive?"

"No. Anyway, my dad's paying, so you can get whatever you want. He's loaded, and I'm sure he won't mind." I grinned.

I spent his money all the time, and he never said a word. A couple of years ago, I stole his credit card. He didn't say anything. When it expired, I found a new one sitting on the kitchen counter. I figured it was his way of giving me money without having to be in the same room with me. He kept me as far away from him as possible, and with my own card, I'd never have to bother him with financial needs.

Right before I left, I'd taken five thousand in cash from his safe. I'd never done that before.

"I want something with chips," Scarlett said.

It took me a second, but I got it—she meant french fries. "Okay, that doesn't really narrow it down because you can get fries with pretty much anything. Are you thinking hamburger or a steak? But I'll tell you, this probably isn't the best place for a steak. They have fish 'n' chips?" She was so thin, maybe she only ate salad. Fries and a salad.

"A burger's fine."

The waitress brought our drinks. "Are you ready to order?"

"Yeah," I said. "I'll have the double bacon cheeseburger."

"And you, miss?"

"I'll have that as well."

The waitress looked at her, I'm sure calculating her size versus where she would put a double bacon cheeseburger. She must have decided it wasn't her problem because she finally nodded and made for the kitchen. More food, more tip.

"So, Scarlett," I said as I took a sip of soda and set my drink to the side, "tell me where you want me to take you." But where she was going didn't interest me nearly as much as what she'd told me in the car. I redirected. "I mean, what were you doing, sneaking into a stranger's car?" She must've been pretty desperate. "You know, something a lot worse than getting left for five minutes on the freeway could have happened."

"I know." She shrank into the depths of my jacket.

"When did you get in? At the gas station or the cemetery?"

"The cemetery." Only with her accent, it came out like "symmetry."

She put a hand on the table and searched for her hot chocolate. The waitress had set it too far away. I moved the mug to the middle of her paper place mat, rotated it so the handle was on her right, and placed her hand on it. Her fingers were icy cold. She wrapped both hands around it.

"Why did you hide in my car?"

She blew on her mug of chocolate. "Dunno. I needed to get away, and yours was the only car I heard."

"So you thought you'd just secretly ride with a stranger to whatever unknown destination he was going to?" Her plan had serious flaws.

"I thought I could hide and then get out at the next stop. Didn't figure it'd be the middle of the motorway, did I?"

"Hey. That wasn't my fault. I said I was sorry."

She took a tentative sip of cocoa.

Could I ask about the kidnapping thing yet? More gently I said, "What happened to you?"

Too soon. She shook her head, and her lip quivered. I could see it, even through her big, dark sunglasses. She was going to cry again.

Switching over to a just-kidding voice, I said, "Anyway, what did you expect, breaking and entering like that? How was I supposed to know you weren't a terrorist or something? I was afraid for my life."

She laughed a little. Crisis averted.

The waitress appeared with our food and clunked the plates on the table in front of us. "Anything else?"

"No, thanks," I said, and she left.

I grabbed the ketchup and squeezed it on my burger. Then squirted a pile for my fries. The hamburger fixings were stacked to the side, trying to trick me into thinking they were something special rather than the restaurant's way of avoiding special orders. I layered on the lettuce, tomato, and pickles, pushed the onions away, then topped it off with the bun. I opened my mouth to eat and glanced at Scarlett. Her food was untouched. I really stank at this.

"Okay," I said, unrolling her silverware from the napkin. She wouldn't need the utensils so I set them aside, but I pressed the napkin into her hand. She laid it on her lap. I named the fixings on her plate, asking if she wanted them all.

"No onions," she said.

"Good choice." I built her a sandwich just like mine. Then I lifted her hand and touched it to her food. "Here's your burger, and here's your fries. Do you want ketchup for your fries?"

"No ketchup. Have they got malt?"

Malt. Not sure what she meant by that, but since the only things on the table were salt, pepper, ketchup, and a sticky pitcher of maple syrup, I assumed no. "Negative. No malt."

"Right." She lifted the burger with surprising skill and took a huge bite.

We ate in silence for a while. She really packed it away. I'd expected a bite or two and then, *Oh no I couldn't; I'm way too full.* But she wolfed it down as fast as I did. Score one for the miniature blind girl.

We neared the end of our meal, and I still knew nothing about her supposed kidnapping or where I should take her. "Now will you tell me how you got here?" I asked. "And what I'm supposed to do with you? If you were kidnapped, shouldn't I take you to the police?"

"No police." She nearly shouted it then cleared her throat. "I already went to them, and there's nothing more they can do."

"Okay." That worked for me. A visit to the police station while leaving town with my dad's money wasn't high on my priority list. "Isn't there someone you know who can help? Somewhere that's home? I could buy you a ticket and send you back to England, to your school?"

"We only go to school till we're sixteen. I have no place there."

"There has to be something. Where did you live after school and before my car?"

"Shh!" she hissed.

Wow. She *really* didn't want to talk about it.

She sat completely still for a moment, and I'm not even sure she took a breath. Then she said, "Christian, where's the loo?"

"The loo?"

"The loo, the toilet, whatever." She sank so low in the booth that her head barely peeked over the top. "Quick. Take me to the toilet."

"Okay, sure." Who was I to argue with a girl's bathroom needs? I took her hand, and she latched onto my arm like it was the only thing keeping her from falling off the face of the planet. I led her to the restroom door, and she pushed it open, dragging me inside.

"Dude," I protested. "This is the girl's bathroom. I'm not coming in with you."

"Are we alone?"

I checked for feet under the stalls, glad that the only person to witness my humiliation couldn't see. "Yeah."

"Christian, listen. I climbed into your car because I needed to get away. They kidnapped me in London and brought me here. I ran away and hid. First in the cemetery, then in your car." She breathed hard, and her pale face grew even whiter. "But he's here. I heard his voice in the restaurant. How did they find me?"

Kidnapped from London and dumped in a Portland cemetery? Unlikely. Plus, if she really was kidnapped, wouldn't the police have shipped her home? And there's no way they—whoever *they* were—could have tracked her here to the restaurant. The only person who saw us together was the airport traffic guard.

Either she was taking me for a ride, or she was crazy. A lunatic. An escapee from the Shepherd Hill School for the Totally Insane. I'd wasted enough time with this pink-haired psycho. Maybe I should let whoever scared her into the bathroom take her home to her padded cell.

I cracked the door and peeked out. Our waitress stood by our table, talking to two men in dark suits. She lifted a napkin, probably looking for money. The men showed her something in a black wallet that looked suspiciously like a police badge. Perfect. Crazy and a criminal. I knew it. I turned to Scarlett.

She groped her way along the bathroom wall, her hands up high, searching for something. A window? There were none.

"I'm gonna go talk to them," I said.

She spun around, her back pressed against the yellow tiled wall. "No."

I left the woman's bathroom—thankfully—and approached our table slowly, listening. I ducked behind a half-size wall topped with fake plants that had faded to an unnatural color of green.

"I don't know," the waitress said. "They were here a minute ago." They all stared at the table—their backs to me—as if by watching long enough, I might materialize out of thin air.

"Did you see them leave? Did you give them a bill?" The man asking the questions was the taller of the two, lanky with light-brown hair. He had a calm, deep voice that came from his throat. "Did you run a credit card?"

"No, they must've left without paying."

I pulled out two twenties then walked over and dropped them on the table. "Sorry about that. I went to get some cash." I motioned toward the ATM machine I'd noticed in the vestibule as we came in.

"Where's the girl?" the shorter cop asked. He had reddish-blond hair and a nasty scar across one eye.

When I saw them close up, they didn't look like cops. The tall man wore a cheap, poorly tailored suit, the other man, a tough-guy leather jacket. They looked like suspects on *America's Most Wanted*. But more than that, they didn't feel right. My guts screamed at me to keep out of it. When I left the bathroom, I'd planned on turning Scarlett in, but it felt like leaving her on the I-205 all over again.

"She left," I said, hopefully in an easy-come, easy-go kind of way. "I gave her some money and put her on a bus."

The tall guy stepped aside and started punching numbers on his phone.

"Which bus?" the one with the scar asked.

I knew nothing about public transit in the greater Portland-Vancouver area. I tried to bluff. "Who are you? Do you have some kind of warrant or license or something? Maybe I should call the cops." I got out my cell phone to show I meant business.

"You don't want to do that," Scarface said. He opened his jacket to reveal a big handgun parked in a shoulder holster. "Which bus?"

I glanced at the waitress. She was stacking our dirty plates and hadn't seen his threat.

I should've left Scarlett on the highway. Well, maybe not on the highway but at least at the airport. This was more mess than I wanted to be involved in. "I don't know. The big one with Portland blinking across the front." Hopefully, *Thou shalt not lie* didn't apply when dangerous-looking men were flashing guns at you.

The tall guy repeated that information into his phone.

"How do you know her?" Scarface asked.

Who were these guys? What could Scarlett possibly have done to have men with guns tracking her? She seemed pretty helpless to me.

"Speak up," he commanded.

"Look, I don't know anything, okay. I found her on the side of the highway. I gave her a meal and money for the bus. That's all. Why? What'd she do?" I doubted they'd tell me anything, but it didn't hurt to try.

He got all concerned-looking and said in a sugary voice, "She ran away from home, and her parents are worried sick."

From London? With no bags or money? How stupid did he think I was? "You know what? I think that's a load of—"

I didn't get to finish because he launched forward and punched me hard in the face.

CHAPTER THREE
CHRISTIAN VS. THE AUDIBLE

I FLEW BACK, CRASHING ONTO the table behind me. I'd never taken a right hook to the jaw before. It hurt a lot more than I expected.

The waitress rushed over. "Hey! That's enough. We answered your questions; now you'd better leave. Or I *am* calling the cops."

The tall man glared at Scarface. "Nice work, Connor," he said as they walked toward the door. "We told you to keep a low profile."

They left the restaurant, and the waitress turned to me. "You okay, kid?"

"Just swell." I rubbed my face where he'd hit me. "Ow."

The waitress pulled a wad of napkins from the stainless-steel dispenser and handed them to me. "You're bleeding."

I dabbed at my lip. He'd cut it when he smacked my jaw. I opened and closed my mouth, making sure I didn't have a broken bone.

"I'll get you some ice." She went to a serving station and filled a plastic cartoon-decorated kiddie cup with ice chips then snapped on a bright red lid. "Sorry, I don't have a bag."

"Thanks," I said, holding the cool relief to the side of my face.

"Sure."

I nodded and walked back to the women's restroom. It was empty. "Scarlett?" I checked under the stalls for the second, and with any luck, last time. Nothing. "You can come out now. They're gone." I pushed open the stall doors, crossing my fingers that some short old lady wasn't sitting on the toilet. I'd be scarred for life.

A woman walked in, saw me, and checked the picture on the door. "I'm almost done," I said, not really sure what that might mean. But she left.

I opened a cupboard under the sink and found Scarlett curled up amidst a stash of scented plug-ins and ammonia glass cleaner.

"They're gone. You wanna come out? Or stay here? It doesn't matter to me." The weird thing is, it kind of did matter. She'd gotten under my skin, and hard as I tried not to, I cared about what happened to her.

She crawled out. "What did you tell them?"

"I told them you took a bus back to the city."

"How did they find me?"

"I don't know. Maybe the traffic guy at the airport." That was a good question. Did they know who I was? Were they following my car? They seemed to accept my story about the bus. But what about Scarlett's story? I'd just taken a fist in the face for her; she owed me the truth. "Let's get out of here."

"Okay." She reached out a hand, and I laid it on my arm.

We left the bathroom and headed for the exit. The waitress watched us for a moment, Scarlett clinging to my arm—wearing sunglasses—inside—at night—and seemed to finally digest Scarlett's disability.

"Hey," I said to the waitress. "I don't really know what's going on. But I have a bad feeling about those men. If they come back, maybe you could pretend you didn't see us leave together?"

She nodded and turned her back.

I paused before opening the front door and scanned the parking lot. A young family made their way toward the restaurant, the parents wrangling their herd of kids toward the entrance. Other than that, the place was quiet. We hurried out to the car, and I did my best to keep us in the shadows, away from the glow of the street lamps. I pulled out of the parking lot, checking repeatedly in the rearview mirror. No one seemed to be following us.

No one seemed to be following us? Those were words I hadn't thought I'd need today when I packed up my stuff and left home. Now I glanced over my shoulder every two seconds. What had this girl gotten herself mixed up in? I'd never make it to Canada tonight. Especially not with documentless Scarlett in tow.

I called an audible. My parents had an old cabin in Hood River. A little A-frame snuggled at the base of Mount Hood. My dad hadn't been there since Mom died, but I went with my buddies on the weekends sometimes. Or by myself when I needed to get away.

I'd take Scarlett there and wait out the night. And in the morning? Well, hopefully I could get more information out of her before then.

I didn't want to backtrack where Scarface and his pal might be lurking. So I took us east on the Washington side of the Columbia River. It'd add a half hour to the trip, but it was safer. At least I assumed. I had no clue what exactly we were running from.

When we passed Camas and merged onto the Lewis and Clark highway, I couldn't wait any longer. The time had come to get some answers.

"Scarlett, you have to tell me what's going on." I drove with one hand on the steering wheel and the other holding the melting-ice cup to my aching jaw. "How am I supposed to help you if you won't tell me the truth? Why are those guys looking for you?"

She squirmed in her seat and shivered. I showed her how to turn on the seat heater.

"I sort of saw something they did," she finally said. "Something bad. I went to the police, but they didn't believe me. Somehow, they must have found out."

"Wait a minute. You *saw* something?" There's no way she'd been faking her blindness.

"The truth is"—she paused for a second then continued in a melodramatic voice—"I see dead people."

I rolled my eyes for her benefit then remembered she couldn't see it. If she'd said that at the restaurant, I would have laughed out loud. But here in the dark, with the green glow of the dashboard reflecting off her sunglasses and illuminating her pale face, it creeped me out.

"Are you telling me you see ghosts?"

She laughed. "No, I'm kidding." She tucked her legs up and circled her arms around them. "But I do sometimes see people who are going to die. Like a vision of the future or something."

"You mean, like a fortune teller?" Maybe she had Braille tarot cards.

All the humor faded from her face. "When I was nine years old, we were poor as church mice. We lived with my grandmother. Mum drank and had a hard time keeping a steady job. Anyway, I loved Gran. She took me to the park and read to me. She saved up all her money so I could have books in Braille." Scarlett ran her knuckles back and forth on the window, making lines she couldn't see in the condensation. Her accent grew stronger the longer she spoke.

"One night, I dreamed she didn't wake up. I shook her and shook her, but nothing happened. Mum was out, and I waited home alone all day. I woke up screaming. Gran came in to comfort me, said it was just a dream and that she would be alive for a long time still.

"A week later, Mum was at work, and I went in to wake up Gran. I wanted breakfast. It happened exactly like my dream. Exactly. She wouldn't wake up. I sat home, alone, all day with my grandmother dead in her bed."

Holy smokes. That would be enough to permanently damage any kid.

"A few months later, I dreamed our landlord got shot by an angry tenant. I told Mum, and she called me a barmy git. Then, guess what?"

I didn't like where this story was going. "Your landlord got shot?"

"Bang on." She slipped her fingers under her glasses and rubbed her eyes. "The police interviewed everyone in the building. I told them about my dream, and they laughed. What would a blind kid know about anything? A few weeks later, I dreamed the landlord's wife hanged herself from the balcony. This time, I kept it to myself. Next day, the police were back at our building cutting down her dead body."

"What about your mom? Didn't she believe you after the landlord?"

"Maybe. But I think it freaked her out. She hit the bottle even harder, and we lived on nothing but my measly government stipend for being blind. That's when social services sent me to Shepherd Hill. After a year or two, Mum came to the Shepherd to say good-bye. She'd taken up with a guy from Amsterdam, and she was leaving to be with him. I haven't heard from her since."

She'd lived a hard life, that's for sure. I hoped her school had treated her better. "And you were at Shepherd Hill until you got kidnapped?"

"No. Had to leave end of last year, didn't I? We finish at sixteen."

"So they dumped you with nowhere to go?" I tried to picture Scarlett living off the streets of London—blind. She must not have done too bad; pink hair and Doc Martins aren't exactly free.

"I had a friend. A bloke I met at the Shepherd—Simon. He works there, one of the administrators. He let me crash at his flat for the summer."

I wasn't sure I really wanted to know what Simon might have asked for in return for free room and board. But I couldn't help myself. "Was he your boyfriend?"

"No. Just a friend."

Right, a friend. How often did that really work out? But we'd gotten off topic. "So why did Scarface take you?"

"Scarface?" she asked.

"The guy, I think his name was Connor; he had a scar across his eye." I drew a line down my own face for demonstration then kicked myself again for being so boneheaded. Would I never get used to the fact that she couldn't see? Until I'd met Scarlett, I'd never realized how much I took sight for granted. I based everything in my life on vision. I couldn't imagine a world of darkness.

"Oh." She cleared her throat. "After I left the Shepherd, I dreamed that one of the other girls was taken and killed. I went to the police and told them my past experience with dreams and what I saw happen to Katie. The gits still didn't believe me. Two weeks later, she vanished. The police came and asked me more questions, details about who did it. But I couldn't describe him in a way that satisfied the investigators. They asked me loads of times about hair color. Don't know colors, do I?"

Probably not. If you've never seen color, how would you? In that case, how would she know anything? What did death look like in the dreams of a blind person?

She took a deep breath and continued. "Next day, some men broke into the flat, put tape on my mouth, and stuffed me in a bag."

I almost swerved off the road. "A bag?" Every word she told me made me sicker and sicker.

"Like a suitcase or gym bag or something."

I clenched the steering wheel. Who did stuff like that? Did she fly in a duffel bag across the Atlantic, wedged into the pressurized cargo hold? Who knew what else they might've done? My bacon double cheeseburger churned in the pit of my stomach. I didn't want to hear any more. I'd seen stuff like this on TV all the time. But having it sitting next to me in the car wrenched my guts.

She wiped her eyes again.

"Don't cry." Anything but crying. "I'm really sorry I was such an idiot before, leaving you on the road."

"It's fine."

"You're safe now. Okay?"

"Yeah." She leaned her head against the window. In a few minutes, her breathing came slow and steady; she'd fallen asleep. She must've been exhausted.

I turned right and crossed the Columbia River back into Oregon on the Bridge of the Gods, stopping at the tollbooth to pay the dollar toll. I watched in my rearview mirror for a set of headlights to follow me across the bridge. None did. They must have gone back to Portland. Thirty minutes later, we passed through Hood River and out into the forest to the cabin at the base of the volcano. The only place I ever found a shred of peace.

When I pulled into the gravel driveway, Scarlett still slept. I left her in the car and went inside. The place was pitch black, and I wanted to get some lights on to check that things were in order before bringing her in.

My grandfather built the home when my mom was young, before she married into the Morris clan, where money grew on the family tree. Grandpa passed it on to my mother.

A black lava rock fireplace divided the main floor in half, with a family room in front and a kitchen and bathroom in back. A narrow staircase led to a loft area with a queen-size bed. Not a lot of rooms, but they'd been updated and were open and spacious. Dad had suggested adding on, making it bigger and more luxurious to match the other homes on the river. Mom had an architect drawing plans when she got sick. Dad never came back.

With the cabin lit up and ready, I went out to get Scarlett.

"Scarlett," I whispered. She didn't stir. I gave her a little shake but got nothing, so I lifted her out of the car. She weighed almost nothing, except her heavy boots, which must have added ten pounds to her miniature body. After hauling her feet around in those things all day, no wonder she was worn out.

I carried her into the cabin, up the stairs, and onto the bed. It took me ten minutes to unlace her boots before I slipped them off and tucked her feet under the covers. Should I take off her dark glasses? Or did that cross too far into invasion of privacy? I left them on. I went downstairs and built a fire to warm the house.

By now I thought I'd be almost to Canada. Or at least spending the night in a nice hotel north of Seattle.

Did my dad even know I was gone? It was just past ten, and he'd be getting home from his office any minute. I'd turned off my phone when I left. With a dexterous kick, I pushed out a chair and took a seat at the warped, pinewood kitchen table. I had four missed calls, seven texts, and three voice messages. I checked the missed calls first. One of the missed calls was from a girl I liked who didn't know I existed—at least that's what I'd thought until I saw her name on my caller ID. I pushed redial, and it went to her voice mail.

"Hi, Beth, it's Christian. I saw you called and so, um, yeah. I'm sorta out of town for a few days." Or the rest of my life, but I didn't want to sever all ties until I knew for sure. A man needs options. This Scarlett thing had thrown a huge wrinkle into my plans. "I guess I'll talk to you later, bye."

I toggled through the rest of the calls. One number I didn't recognize, and the last was from my dad. He'd never called me on my phone before. I didn't even know he knew my number. But it's not like I ever called him either. We had mastered the art of noncommunication.

The texts were all from friends: *the new girl is hot . . . Mr. Cooper's homework is lame . . . are you going to the football game tomorrow?* That last was from Jay, my closest friend and the star wide receiver on the football team. He hated when I missed his games. He thrived on glory and praise, and if I didn't show up to feed it to him, he might actually starve.

The feeling was reciprocal. If not for Jay Jackson, I'd be curled up in the fetal position on the basement floor. No one besides Jay and his father knew the truth about my life in purgatory. In fact, most kids envied me. Money, car, no parental interference. From the outside, it looked ideal. From the inside, it burned me up. No pat on the back when I did something well. No swat on the butt to keep me in line. No one to care if I lived or died. Being left alone is not at all what it's cracked up to be. So, Jay. He fastened me onto his safety line and dragged me forward—no matter how hard I kept slipping back.

I was ninety-nine percent sure his dad, the bishop, made him do it. At least in the beginning. A special assignment to help the stray find his way back into the fold. Scary thing is, it worked. Jay was cool and friendly, and all the girls swooned after him for his athletic body and his rich, brown skin. He was by far the best thing in my life.

After Mom died, Dad turned his back on the Church and turned instead to work, expensive wine, and severing all ties to his son. Consequently, I went through a pretty rough phase myself—doing everything wrong I could think of to get my father's attention.

I guess that's when Jay's dad made me Project of the Year. I hated it at first, but it didn't take long before I felt relieved that at least one person cared. Jay somehow managed to turn me around, schlepping me to church and forcing me to wake up at the crack of dawn for early-morning seminary.

Bishop Jackson made a valiant effort to save my dad. He came by the house a few times, but Dad never let him past the entryway. The last time he stopped by, my father met him on the porch. It was late, because that's the only time you can catch Richard Morris at home. He left the front door open, and I listened from the top of the stairs as my father berated the bishop for caring, demanding he never speak to him of the Church, God, or his son ever again. That's when I heard my father say, "Christian is free to do whatever he wants. He means nothing to me anymore."

Nothing. The word knotted itself around my neck and tried to strangle me. I was fifteen. I already knew how he felt, but hearing it spoken out loud, to the bishop . . . that was hard. When I told Jay what I'd heard my dad say, he sat in stunned silence for a full five minutes before stoically rising and punching a hole through the wall of his bedroom.

"Sorry I'll miss your game, buddy," I whispered.

His wasn't the only game I'd miss. Jay had convinced me to join the tennis team this year, and I'd be MIA for my own match too.

I dialed my voice mail, but the first message was blank—the unidentified phone number. Whoever had called had hung up without saying anything.

The second message was Jay's. "Dude, where are you? Flaky much? I thought we were going for tacos." I laughed out loud then stopped, remembering Scarlett was sleeping upstairs.

The other message was the one from my dad. "Son, it's your father." Son? When did he ever call me that? Had he finally forgotten my name? "I'm worried about you. Call me." Worried? About me? Not likely. Worried about the stolen money, I'd bet. And no thanks on the *call me* option. That was a tie I was willing to sever.

I shoved the phone into my pocket and grabbed a pillow and a sleeping bag from the closet. The scraping of the sliding door sounded loud in the quiet of the night as I headed out to the backyard. I had an old hammock out there, and it was my favorite place to sleep—when it wasn't raining. I unclipped and tossed off the weathered tarp that kept the bird droppings at bay and unrolled the sleeping bag. It was made for arctic temperatures, and within two minutes of snuggling in, I was already getting hot. I unzipped it a foot or two and tried to relax.

Images from the day whizzed through my mind like cars passing me on the freeway. Dead grandmas, landladies swinging from the balcony, and my father opening his safe and finding half his money gone. Maybe not half, but I took a lot.

When I finally slept, I dreamed about a girl with pink hair standing in the middle of a sea of speeding cars. The cars honked and swerved, always missing her at the last second. Then she screamed. I sat up so fast I spun off the hammock and hit the ground.

I heard the scream again, faint and distant. It took me three ragged breaths to realize where I was and that the scream did not come from my dream but from Scarlett inside the cabin.

CHAPTER FOUR

CHRISTIAN VS. MOUNT HOOD

I FOUGHT MY WAY OUT of the sleeping bag, a feat that would have amazed even the Great Houdini. With a heavy swoosh, I threw open the sliding door and took the stairs two at a time. Images of a man up there packing Scarlett into a suitcase raced through my mind.

When I reached the loft, Scarlett cried out again, jerking her head back and forth. She lay curled on her side, facing away from me. I shook her shoulder. "Scarlett. Wake up."

She stilled. Her sunglasses rested at an awkward angle across her face. I envisioned her eyes snapping open under their coverings. If they opened at all.

She rolled onto her back and moaned. "Where am I?"

I sat on the edge of the huge bed. "We're at my cabin, at Mount Hood."

"Christian?"

"Yeah?"

"What happened?"

"Nothing. You fell asleep, and I put you in bed." Did she think I'd been . . . inappropriate? "Then you screamed in your sleep, so I woke you up. Did you have another death dream?"

She sat up and straightened her glasses. With her head tipped a little to the side, she said, "Feels dark. What time is it?"

"About one thirty in the morning. How did you know?"

She combed her fingers through her hair, flattening down the back with surprising skill. "I can usually tell day and night and find the sun when it's not cloudy. Or find the source of a very bright light. Mostly by warmth."

I guess that made sense. I craved a computer to look up what I should know about blindness. My ignorance shamed me. I had my laptop in my car but no Internet at the cabin.

"Is there a loo?"

"Yes," I said. "We have a bathroom."

She let out a breath that sounded suspiciously like mockery. "When I need a bath, I ask for the bathroom. When I need a toilet, I ask for the loo."

"Got it." I stood and took her hand, helping her off the bed.

She hooked her fingers around my arm. "You're tall, yeah?"

"Six-two. But, then, everyone must be tall from your perspective."

"Hey, easy on the short people." She released my arm and stepped around to face me. "Can I touch you?"

I assumed she meant my face, to know what I looked like. At least, that's what I'd always seen in the movies, and I was pretty much basing everything I knew about vision-impaired people on what Hollywood had taught me.

"Hang on," I said. "Unlike you, I need the lights." I flipped the switch at the top of the stairs and lit the room.

I wanted to see her face. Her eyes. Not out of some morbid curiosity, but because people always say that the eyes are the windows to the soul. With her glasses on, I had a hard time reading her. If I looked into her eyes, could I see her soul? "Tell you what. I'll make you a deal. You can touch me *if* you take your shades off."

"Deal." She removed the glasses and tossed them on the bed behind her. Nicely done. She faced me again, and her gaze—if she'd had one—fell on the collar of my rumpled T-shirt. I lifted her chin. They looked like regular eyes, light brown and clear. I guess I'd expected cloudy or half closed or something.

They stared back at me, but they were blank. It was obvious they didn't see me. They weren't the windows I'd hoped for. But still, they drew me in. She had a pretty face, especially without the big, dark glasses blocking half of it.

"Well?" she asked.

"Very nice."

She blushed a little. "No. I meant, is it my go?"

"Sure."

She put her hands on my arms then moved them up and felt my shoulders. I tried to resist the urge to flex, but I couldn't stop myself. I had some okay muscles, so why not show them off? I tensed just enough to firm up my biceps and deltoids.

Scarlett shook her head. "Guys. You're all the same." Stepping close, she reached up and ran her hands through my hair. Her breath tickled my neck.

She felt my face next, letting her fingers run softly across my eyebrows and eyes, cheeks, nose, and last, my mouth.

No man, no matter the circumstances, can stand in front of an attractive girl and be touched like that and not be affected by it. My heart sped up, and I felt suddenly warm, even though the fire had burned out.

Her fingertips lingered on my mouth, on the swollen and cut lip. "What happened here?"

"Oh, uh." I exhaled, releasing the pressure that had been building in my lungs. "That guy in the restaurant punched me. I'm fine."

Her hands dropped. "I'm sorry I got you mixed up in this. My life's a mess. I didn't mean to bung it on you."

I knew I should say something, but I was still thinking about her fingertips on my mouth.

"Tell me about the house," she said.

Yes, a distraction. "Well, my grandfather built it. It's an old A-frame—"

"No. I mean give me the layout. So I can get around better."

"Oh, right." I placed her hand back on my arm and described the cabin, walking her through the rooms and letting her touch the couch, the glasses and sink, and anything else I thought she might need. Then I deposited her in the bathroom—I mean, the *loo*—and left her alone so she could do whatever she needed to do.

I sat down on the couch, waiting to make sure she was all right before going back out to my hammock. She came out of the bathroom a minute later and walked into the main room, running her hand along the pine wall paneling until she came to the stairs.

"You okay?" I asked.

"Lovely."

"All right. I'll be out back if you need anything."

"Outside?"

"Yeah." I stood up and made my way to the door. "I like it out there. Plus, boy. Girl. Alone. I don't do that. I have . . . boundaries."

She stared into space for a minute. "A gentleman, are you? I s'pose that's cool." She climbed the stairs.

Gentleman? I'd never been called that before. It was better than the usual *old-fashioned*. "Hey, kill the lights, would ya?"

She stopped at the top of the stairs.

"About three feet ahead, on the left."

She ran her hand forward along the wall and took a step.

"A little higher."

She raised her arm and brushed the switch plate. Before she flipped it, she turned and smiled at me.

* * *

I woke to the sound of Scarlett knocking on the sliding door window.

"Hullo out there."

This time, I managed to extract myself from the sleeping bag without the whole flopping-on-the-ground thing. When I opened the door, she leaned against the frame with her arms crossed. Her hair was damp and smelled like men's aftershave.

"Hi," I said through a yawn.

"I hope you don't mind that I showered. I used your shampoo."

"No problem. You smell good." *Wait, did I just say that?*

"Thanks." She didn't seem to think it was weird that I appreciated clean man smell. "I'm starving, and there's nothing to eat."

"Yeah, we don't come here much. Give me a second to shower, and we'll head into town for supplies." I slipped past her and into the house. On the table lay the bag of corn nuts I'd bought on my way out of the city. I tossed them to her. It hit her in the chest and fell to the ground. Oops. "Uh, you can snack on these," I said, picking them up and placing them in her hand.

I led her back into the family room, and she sat on the couch, fumbling to find the sealed end of the corn nuts bag. When she finally opened it, she smelled it and wrinkled her nose then popped one in her mouth. She chewed a few times. "It's very crunchy."

Thirty minutes later, we drove into Hood River—a quaint town that served as the hub for all of the recreational traffic in the area. Windsurfers on the Columbia, skiers on the volcano. There was a small grocery store by the highway, where we came in. Scarlett wasn't wearing her sunglasses, and she had her face turned up, soaking in the warmth that came in through the sunroof.

We wandered through the store's aisles, me pushing the wobbly shopping cart and Scarlett holding my arm, always walking a half step behind. I'd name various foods, and she'd say if something sounded good. I don't know why, but for some reason, I never tired of hearing her British accent. I loved the way her voice bounced up at the end of her questions.

I dumped our loot onto the conveyor belt. The checkout lady stared at me a second then asked, "What happened to your face?"

"Someone gave my friend a hard time." I tipped my head in Scarlett's direction.

"You sure showed him," the lady said dryly.

Scarlett snorted beside me.

While we drove back to the cabin, Scarlett snacked on Twinkies. "These are disgusting," she said, tearing the plastic off another two-pack.

"Then wait for breakfast."

"Don't you fret. I'll still be hungry."

My phone vibrated in my pocket. Another message. I doubted it was my dad again. He'd already surpassed his lifetime phone-call quota. It was Jay. I ignored it. *Sorry, man.*

But the call made me wonder about Scarlett. "Do you want to use my phone?" I offered. "To call someone, Simon or whoever, and tell them you're safe?" I hadn't even thought about this last night, especially after Connor and his buddy had left their mark. It surprised me that she hadn't asked for the phone before now. There must be someone wondering where she was.

"Sure."

I turned on the phone and handed it to her, touching it to the back of her hand. She took it and ran her fingers across the face.

"I can't use this," she said. "It's a touch screen."

Duh. No buttons to feel. I took it and asked her what the number was. I had to pull over and look up the country code for the United Kingdom, but we figured it out, and I dialed it for her. She didn't say who the number belonged to.

She held the phone to her ear for a minute then said, "He's not answering."

So she did call Simon. "Do you have another number?"

She rattled off a different one.

I dialed it, pushed send, and gave her the phone again. When I heard a faint *hullo* on the other end, I started driving.

"Hullo, Joannie? It's Scar. I just wanted to let you know that I'm out of town for a bit, but I'm fine, and I'll call you when I get home. Ta." She passed me my phone. "She didn't answer either. I left a message."

"Okay." That was it? Two people who worried about a vanished girl? Maybe in some ways, her life wasn't all that different from mine. Did she feel as abandoned as I did? Totally alone?

I turned into the lane leading up to the cabin and slowed. The tail end of an older-model, black Chevy Tahoe stuck out beyond the trees that shaded our driveway.

"Scarlett, someone's at the cabin. Pull your hood up." She still wore my jacket, and she recoiled into it.

Was it the tall guy and his fist-happy friend, Connor? How did they find us? Maybe it wasn't them. But who else would be at the cabin? Dad? Not a chance—and it wasn't his car. He'd said he was worried. Would he have sent someone to get me? Never. It had to be the same guys from the restaurant.

I figured we'd be less conspicuous driving past nonchalantly than stopping and reversing down the narrow road, or worse, attempting a six point U-turn. My tinted windows would conceal us if they were watching the road. But if they'd found me at Shari's, they must recognize my car. Scarlett sank down in her seat, and I drove past a little too fast. I kept my head facing forward while my eyeballs wrenched out of their sockets to watch the house. The front door was closed, and other than the Tahoe, everything looked just like we'd left it.

I drove about a hundred yards up the road and pulled into a driveway, concealing the Rover behind the neighbor's storage shed. "Did you leave anything in the cabin?" I asked Scarlett.

"Like what? My skivvies? Or do you mean my Louis Vuitton suitcase with loads of nice clothes?"

Sheesh. Thanks for the rain of sarcasm. "I mean something that would tell them you've been here." If they didn't have proof she was there, maybe they'd take their search back to Portland. "Where are your sunglasses?"

"Here." She pulled them out of the jacket pocket and put them on. "I didn't leave anything. Haven't got anything to leave, have I?"

"Fine. You stay here. I'm gonna see what they're up to." I quietly opened my car door.

"No. Don't go."

Even with her dark lenses covering half her face, I could see her fear. "Hey, I'll be right back. I'm not gonna talk to them." I rubbed my swollen jaw, remembering how well that had worked out last time. "I'll just sneak in for a closer look." I handed her the keys. "You'd better keep these just in case."

"In case I need to drive the getaway car?"

For crying out loud! Could I be more stupid? I tried to salvage what was left of my intelligence—which wasn't much. "In case you need to lock the car or something. The lock button is the top left." I slipped out and closed the door, waiting until I heard the locks click.

I slunk through the woods, back toward my cabin, keeping low and sticking to the areas with heavy underbrush. When the house came into view, I hid behind a huge tree trunk and peeked around through the branches. I had a good view of the front yard and driveway. A faded sticker on the car's bumper read, *Someone in Oregon Loves Me.* Who could that possibly be? His mother?

The tall man from Shari's rounded the side of the house. He'd replaced his lame suit with casual clothes: jeans and an outdoorsy, moleskin jacket. He looked more like a model for some men's casual wear magazine than a kidnapper. He opened the cabin door and called in, "You find anything, Connor?" His voice was deep and smooth.

Connor stepped out of the house holding up two limp towels, one in each hand. "How many guys you know use two towels when they shower?"

Shoot! I'd forgotten about those. It didn't prove anything, except that these idiots were smarter than I thought. Smart enough to figure an unmade bed *and* a sleeping bag crumpled on the hammock, plus two wet towels, could only mean one thing.

I toyed with the idea of approaching them again and dishing out another lie. I met my girlfriend here, or my buddy and me were going fishing and I came back because I forgot my net. But I'd have to go back to my car to make anything believable. And they'd likely just hit me again.

"Let's go," the tall guy said.

Connor shook his head. "They might come back. We should wait here."

"Why? So you can overreact again? We didn't hire you to take out everyone that gets in our way." He tossed the wet towels into the cabin. "That's not what this is about. You're going to jeopardize everything if you don't calm down."

Who's he *taking out*? Did he mean me? Or Scarlett? Or had he already taken someone out?

"Ha!" Connor said, using his foot to wipe out a footprint in the mud made by the other guy when he came around the house. "You would be lost without me."

The tall guy didn't answer. But for a second, it looked like he might punch Connor.

I watched them for a couple more minutes while they conferred together. They spoke more quietly this time, and I caught only parts of what they said. "Who tipped him off?" "How much does he know?" "Is he heading back to his house?" "His father . . ." That was the last I heard before they got in their car and drove away.

They went to my dad. That's how they knew about the cabin. Somehow, they'd figured out who I was and connected me to my father. Did Dad take one look at those thugs and decide good-bye and good riddance, telling them all the information they'd needed to track me down and rid himself of me forever?

What about Scarlett? What did they want from her? If they wanted her dead, they could have taken care of that in London. Why drag her halfway around the world? I didn't dare leave her alone any longer. I started back toward the car, cutting through the woods to avoid walking out in the open.

I was in way over my head. How could I protect someone from guys like that? I had no idea. Again, I fell back on my Hollywood education. Jason Bourne would've walked up and killed them both with the wet towels. They didn't teach those skills in boys PE. They taught badminton and bowling. If only I'd had a ten-pound bowling ball, I could've knocked 'em right over.

When I reached the car, it was empty. The doors were unlocked, and the keys lay on the cargo holder between the front seats.

"Scarlett," I called.

No answer.

CHAPTER FIVE

CHRISTIAN VS. THE SHOPPING TRIP

"SCARLETT?" I RAKED MY HANDS through my hair. "Scarlett!"

They must've seen me drive by after all. And when they found the towels . . .

"Scarlett!" I studied the fallen leaves on the gravel driveway, looking for signs of a struggle. The only thing I made out were tire tracks leading to my Range Rover. But what did I know about tracking? Once again, my education failed me. I was now one hundred percent convinced that schools in America did nothing to prepare kids for life in the real world.

"Scarlett!" I screamed. A dozen birds flapped out of a tree and took to the sky, raining golden leaves on my head.

I checked behind and under all the seats in my car. I searched the woods surrounding the neighbor's place and my cabin, all the while calling and calling. I rattled the door of the shed. Locked. I stepped back and kicked it as hard as I could, right next to the handle. The door crashed open. The sudden release of energy felt good. Scarlett wasn't there.

"No, *no*, NO!" I'd watched them drive away in the opposite direction. How did they get her? I paced back and forth, clenching and unclenching my fists. The layer of fallen leaves muffled the crunch of my feet stomping on the gravel driveway.

An old-fashioned metal garbage can stood against the side of the house. I hauled my leg back to kick it all the way to the top of Mount Hood. But I didn't. I lifted the lid. There was Scarlett. Huddled in the bottom, her head on her knees, hands covering her ears.

I swallowed hard. "What are you doing?"

Her face turned up toward the sound of my voice.

"Didn't you hear me calling?"

"I heard you. The people in China heard you."

"Then why didn't you answer?" She'd given me a heart attack for no reason. I lifted her out of the can and set her on the ground.

"What if they're still here?"

I shook my head. "They're gone. I saw them both get in their car and drive away."

She stood still, her head bent down. "I didn't."

No. Of course not. She might have heard a car leave. But what did that tell her about who might have stayed behind? Or who might be lurking in the forest.

I reached out and pulled her into my arms. It was like hugging a fencepost, only warm and soft and curvy. Maybe I'd overstepped my bounds, but she didn't push me away. Instead, she put her arms around my waist and sort of squeezed. It had been so long since anyone had hugged me. "I'll make you a deal. I promise I will never call you out of hiding unless I know it's totally safe if you promise to answer."

"Deal."

"You scared the mess out of me." But I figured she already knew that, considering her ear was pressed up against my chest, listening to my heart pound away.

"Sorry," she said.

I helped her back into the Rover. "I don't think we should stay here. They could come back. Or they might have bugged it, waiting for us."

"Okay. Where to?"

I shrugged. "These guys are persistent. We can't run forever. They'll find us. They'll find you." I'd already proven that I stank at keeping her safe. "I think we should tell the police."

"No way." She shook her head. "Tried that, didn't I? And it didn't do a bit of good. I already told you, that's how this whole thing started. I dreamed about Katie and went to the police. Then, when Katie actually disappeared, the police came back, asking me questions. It's not coincidence that the next day the kidnappers came after me." She was shouting now. "So, you can just leave me here, because I won't go. I won't." She turned her head away and felt for the door handle.

I locked the doors so she couldn't escape and leaned my head back on the seat rest. Stubborn punk Brit-girl. "Fine. Have it your way." I let out a loud sigh, careful to add extra exasperation on the exhale. "Scarlett, you have to tell me what they want. Do you know them?"

"No. I don't know them, or I would have given their names to the police in London, wouldn't I? And I don't know what they want."

There had to be something in all of this to help me understand why they were searching for Scarlett. "What about the dream? Can you give me more details about that? Do you know if the men in your dream are the same as the ones in the restaurant and snooping around the cabin?"

"Maybe. Describe them to me." It sounded like a reasonable request, but in her voice, I sensed a challenge. She was testing me. But about what?

"One was tall with light-brown hair." I paused. Okay, I got it now. She wanted me to prove I was worthy of associating with a blind girl. I closed my eyes and recreated the scene in the restaurant, since that's when she'd said she recognized one of their voices. I tried to block out any visual aids and focused on the other senses.

I started over. "One was tall, taller than me." Maybe she could sense height based on voice direction, so I kept that in. "His voice was deep and throaty, like he had a cold or something, but also soothing, like the voice-over for movie trailers." What else? "Um . . . Oh! He smelled like Old Spice." I knew 'cause Jay wore it too. "And he chewed gum, so there might have been some mint scent, but I didn't smell it myself." I'd covered sound and smell. Taste? I couldn't help her there. All I tasted was blood in my mouth after Scarface hit me.

That left me with touch. "He wore a cheap suit, so his clothes would've been rough, like polyester." Rough clothes?—totally lame. What a bunch of useless garbage. Just because he chewed gum and wore a suit in the restaurant doesn't mean he did in Scarlett's dream.

I looked over at her, and she was covering her mouth, trying not to giggle. "Shut up," I said.

She let it all out and laughed even harder. When she finished and wiped her eyes, she said, "Actually, that was brilliant. Probably the best anyone's ever done. Especially after such a short time."

I gave myself a pat on the back. Another wasted gesture because she couldn't see it. If she only knew how many times I'd blundered, she wouldn't be so liberal with her praise.

I guess I passed the test because she got serious again and said, "In my dream, there are three people, plus Katie, my friend from the Shepherd. They're in a room with a hard, smooth floor. Katie lies on a bed with a cold metal top, no mattress or blankets. A bright light shines on her face, making it warm to the touch. The other three people surround the bed. There is a rolling tray to the side, filled with small tools. When I run my hands over them, they remind me of silverware, but heavy for their size. The tools clink and clatter as they are used and exchanged for others.

"The room smells like medicine and surgical spirit. One person is female. She's tall for a woman and wears glasses. Her hair is pulled up in a knot on her head. 'We failed,' she says, and her voice is deep and soft, like lying on a bed of cotton fluff, but full of disappointment. The other two are men. One, I think, is the man with the scar; when I touch his face, I feel the mark. The other man fades away, and I wake before I can know him." By the time she finished speaking, all remnants of laughter and joking were gone.

How did she glean all of that from a dream when she had no vision? Maybe she could see in her dreams. Or maybe she saw the dream world clearly but within her own scope of sensory perception. She'd painted a perfect picture of some kind of medical procedure gone awry. "What did they do to Katie?"

She didn't answer. Instead, she leaned forward and covered her face with her hands.

"Don't cry." I reached over and put my hand on her back, rubbing in gentle circles.

"In my dream, I touch her face. It's sticky and wet. Smells like blood. Her eyes hang loose out of their sockets."

My hand froze. "Was Katie blind?"

"No, she wasn't. *Isn't*. She could still be alive, right?" She broke down again, her body shaking.

"Sure. She could be fine." But I doubted it. If they were this tenacious about finding Scarlett, I didn't have much hope for Katie. That is, assuming the whole dream-becomes-reality thing was true. "What were they doing to her?"

She shook her head. "Dunno."

I rubbed her back for a second longer, until she lifted her wet face from her hands. Then I said, "Okay, let's get going."

She sort of nodded, and I thought I heard a soft, "'Kay."

I backed out of the neighbor's driveway. When we passed my cabin, the front door was only half closed. I stopped the car and opened my door.

"Where are you going?" she cried, her hand latching onto my arm.

"It's fine. I'm just going to lock up. I'll be two seconds." I hurried to the house and secured the dead bolt then jogged back to the car.

We couldn't stay here. And I wouldn't go home. I'd never get into Canada with Scarlett, not legally anyway. I had no idea how to attempt an undercover border crossing, so that ruled out my aunt's house.

"Okay. Here's the plan"—at least the best plan I could come up with—
"I'll take you back to Portland. We can hang out there for a few hours, blend
into the crowd, until this Simon guy answers his phone. Then we'll figure out a
way to get you on a plane back to London. Will he meet you at the airport?"

She nodded. "I think so. Or I can take the tube."

I dialed his number and passed the phone to Scarlett.

"He's still not picking up," she said.

Shoot. I could give her some money to pay for a taxi when she got to
the London airport. Maybe I could throw in some extra. I had a couple
grand, but was it enough to get her back on her feet? To help her move out
of Simon's apartment? They must have assisted living places for people with
disabilities, and she'd mentioned a government stipend. Would the men who'd
searched the cabin go all the way back to England to kidnap her again? It was
hard to believe they'd gone to all that trouble to kidnap her just because she
dreamed about a murder. It didn't seem like she posed that much of a threat.

After a quick stop at a fast-food drive-thru, we merged onto the
highway, backtracking west toward Portland.

"Scarlett, where were you when you found my car? Before the cemetery?
If I knew how you got away from them and into my car, maybe we can find
out who is behind all this."

I hoped that if I had something solid, some real evidence, I could
convince Scarlett to go to the police. I'd already proven I was no Jason
Bourne. These were problems for professionals—CIA, FBI—whoever
solved nasty crimes that spanned two continents. If I couldn't get her
home soon, I'd have to go to the police whether she wanted to or not. But
if we could figure out who had taken her, maybe the police would be more
willing to listen and do something about it.

"When they put me in the suitcase, they must've drugged me," she said.
"When I woke up, I was inside a locked room. Sometimes being blind
pays off, because the gits did nothing to secure the windows. I waited until
dark—it wasn't long—then crawled out."

"How did you know you wouldn't fall five stories to your death?" It
seemed like a big risk. But maybe that was a gamble she was willing to make
rather than end up on the operating table.

"I smelled grass and mulch and felt coolness from the earth on my face."

The kidnappers weren't the only ones to underestimate the blind girl—
though I hated lumping myself in with them. She continually surprised me
with her ability to use her other senses to navigate the darkness of her world.

"I went in the direction of quiet. I walked for a long time, until I found myself in a cemetery. I hid as best I could, not knowing for certain if I was totally concealed. Then I heard your car, and I figured, why not? It couldn't be worse."

She wrenched the knife stuck in my guilty heart, twisting it relentlessly. "You mean until I dumped you on the interstate? I know I said this already, but I really am sorry about that."

"I know. It's over, and you've made up for it, and more."

"Sure."

She leaned her head back and lifted her face toward the sun again. She seemed to like that. I turned on the stereo and selected a playlist. At the very least, I could try to do something that might bring her a little happiness before I sent her home. Something fun. What would a British punk girl like?

I considered stopping at Multnomah Falls for some sightseeing but quickly decided that was a worthless idea. Then I remembered her comment about not having anything to leave behind back at the cabin. I could take her shopping. Didn't all girls love that? How many days had she been wearing those same clothes? I shuddered.

"How long have you been gone?"

"Dunno for sure, but I'm thinking four or five days. I'm not certain how long I stayed in the bag."

She definitely deserved a diversion. "I'm thinking we should go shopping." There was a Nordstrom at the Lloyd Center Mall in downtown Portland. We could stop there.

The ride from Hood River took a little over an hour. I parked in the lower level of the mall's huge garage. After consulting the store directory, I took Scarlett to the teens department on the second floor. She clung to my arm while we rode the escalator, grinning the whole way up.

I knew nothing—*nothing*—about shopping for girls. I went straight to a sales lady and said, "Hi, this is my friend Scarlett. Her luggage didn't make it. Can you please help her find whatever she wants?"

The sales lady seemed a little old to be working in juniors. But she smiled and tossed her long, dark hair behind her and said, "Of course." She looked like she spent a bit too much time down at the make-up counter. A smudge of red lipstick on her teeth distracted me for a moment.

Scarlett tugged on my arm, and I leaned down. "Are you sure this is okay?" she whispered.

"It's more than okay. Really. Anything you want. Just promise me one thing."

"What?"

"Get some new shoes. Those boots weigh more than you do."

"Promise."

The sales lady, Colette, according to her name tag, led us around the floor. She caught on quickly to Scarlett's blindness, describing the clothing with great detail. She described the jeans, shirts, and sweaters—which Scarlett insisted were actually called "jumpers." Scarlett listened to every word, running her hands over the garments while Colette spoke.

I was about to tell Colette that Scarlett had no concept of color, but then Scarlett snuggled her cheek into a woolly cardigan and asked, "What color is it?"

"You told me you don't know colors," I said.

"I like to hear it anyway."

I wondered again what the world was like from inside her head. The sweater was gray. Did that mean everything soft and fuzzy was gray?

After they'd collected a mound of clothes, I hoped we might be done. But instead of heading to the cashier's counter, Colette steered us toward the dressing rooms.

"Ooh, no," I said, shaking my head. "I am *not* going in there." The women's bathroom had been bad enough. "I'll wait here." I sat on a chair outside. A man sitting across from me cast me a sympathetic look.

Colette took Scarlett into the dressing rooms but then came right back out again. She laughed. "She sent me out for some skivvies."

Oh yeah. No way was I going anywhere near that dressing room. I scooted my chair farther from the entrance then pulled out my phone to check my messages. When I saw three voice mails from my dad, my eyebrows slowly crept up. I pushed play: "Son"—again with the son?—"please call me." *Beep.* "Christian, some men came to the office last night asking about you." Yeah, and you led them right to me. "Call me." *Beep.* "Look, I know you think I don't care." He was wrong. I didn't *think* he didn't care; I *knew* he didn't care. But his voice strained as he finished the message. "I'm worried. Are you in trouble? Call me." He hadn't given me or my life a second thought in years. I shook my head. What a sham.

I had two other messages from the same unidentified caller as last night. Both were just a few seconds of nothing, same as before. I pushed the call back button, and the phone rang.

A man answered. "Hello?"

I knew that voice. It was Deepthroat, or whatever his real name was. The tall guy. I didn't respond.

"Christian Morris," he said with satisfaction, like now that I'd called him, his life was complete.

Betrayed by the caller ID. "Leave Scarlett alone," I said, and hung up. As if that would do any good. Maybe I should've said *pretty please*. I stashed my phone back in my pocket. Idiots. Still, my hands were shaking.

I glanced toward the dressing room door and wished I hadn't. Some lady wearing a pair of jeans that were way too tight was admiring her reflection in the full-size mirror. I looked away quickly, only to find myself staring at a rack of what Scarlett would call *skivvies*. I lowered my eyes to the vacant chair beside me. There was a stack of magazines. I leafed through them—they were all women's stuff. I groaned and tossed them away.

How could it take so long? It's not like she was looking at herself in the mirror. Another lady approached the changing rooms with a stack of clothing. I almost smiled at her, just trying to be friendly. But I didn't. Strange kid hanging around outside the dressing room, watching the women come and go? Kinda creepy.

I rested my head in my hands and studied the orange-gold carpet. I spent the next forever trying to decide if the grayish stain between my feet looked more like a gun or a machete. Either one would've satisfied my growing desire to kill myself rather than sit here a minute longer.

Scarlett finally emerged from the dressing room wearing an outfit consisting of a long black sweater thing and new grungy jeans that hugged her legs all the way to her ankles. A long, thin belt with silver studs looped twice around her hips.

"Well? How'd I do?" she asked.

My mouth went dry. She'd managed to turn her punk look into some-thing . . . hot. I mean, she was good looking before, but . . .

Collette cleared her throat.

Eyes up top, Morris, I reminded myself. "You look very cool."

"Thank you," she said in a voice that implied she already knew she looked good.

Who taught her that? I wanted to know. Colette in the changing room? Or her platonic roommate, Simon?

After getting some sweats for sleeping and a pair of useful shoes—black and gray plaid canvas slip-ons—we were ready to pay. I couldn't convince her to get a jacket.

"I like to wear yours."

"Why?" I asked. "It drowns you."

"I like the way it smells."

Hopefully, that meant clean laundry smell. I actually couldn't remember when I washed it last, and it could've just as easily smelled like BO.

Colette rang up the clothes, and I paid with a wad of my dad's cash. I didn't want to use the credit card because I thought Connor could trace it. I'd ditched them in Hood River, and there was no way they could find me here. I wanted to keep it that way. For all they knew, we could be in Idaho.

Colette handed me our bags and finally—freedom. Whether Scarlett intended to or not, she had at last gotten revenge on me for leaving her on the highway. *Note to self: Do not take a girl shopping ever again.*

Scarlett, on the other hand, smiled bigger than ever, so maybe it had been worth it. She walked with a bounce, but that could've been because I carried her combat boots in one of the bags hanging on my arm.

We passed the skating rink located in the center of the mall, and Scarlett stopped. "Feels cold. What's that sound?"

I started to explain but then figured, why not? "Scarlett, I'm taking you ice skating."

CHAPTER SIX

CHRISTIAN VS. MODERN ART

THE SKATING RINK OCCUPIED THE main courtyard of the bottom floor of the mall. A bridge, frosty blue to look like a walkway of ice, connected the two hallways on the second story above the center of the rink. Iron trestles crisscrossed the ceiling of the Lloyd Center, supporting arched panels of glass that gave the shoppers a view of the sky.

I stuffed Scarlett's bags of new clothes into a locker then got her fitted with a pair of worn white skates. I took a pair of black skates.

"Have you ever been skating before?" I asked, checking her laces one last time.

"Never."

She clung to my arm with both hands while we inched our way onto the ice. I stood in place for a few minutes, letting her find her balance on the thin metal blades. She slid her feet back and forth then bent down and ran her hand along the ice. Her fingertips came up glistening from the cold surface.

"Ready to go?" I asked.

"Chocks away, I s'pose." She laughed.

"Chocks away?"

"You know, off we go. Ready or not."

"Yeah. Sure."

I started off slowly, and she dragged along behind. I supported her entire weight with my arm until she got her feet under her. She caught on quickly, and soon we were skating around the rink at a smooth, easy pace, our blades clacking rhythmically on the ice.

She loved it, laughing and holding her free arm out at graceful angles— something that must come naturally to certain people because she didn't learn it from watching the Olympics. She kept her other arm padlocked around mine, still relying on me for the bulk of her balance. Her cheeks and the tip of her nose flushed pink from the cold, and she looked more alive than ever before.

My phone rang in my pocket, and I checked the ID. It was the unidentified caller who I'd now identified as Deepthroat. Why would he call? I maneuvered us to the side rail and answered.

"Christian?" he asked.

I didn't respond for several seconds. "Maybe," I said and immediately regretted it. Why was I so stupid? He knew it was me. But I had no clue what to say. I'd never been involved in furtive phone calls before. Not even to find out who liked who. We took care of all that stuff with texting.

Still silence.

"Who is this?" I made an effort to sound tough.

"Give us the girl and no one will get hurt."

His line was even more cliché than mine. And more untruthful. "You mean, no one except for Scarlett."

Scarlett listened intently while I spoke. Her smile disappeared like it had been wiped off by the Zamboni. I leaned down so she could hear both sides of the conversation.

"What makes you think that?" Deepthroat asked.

Then it hit me. He was stalling to keep me on the line. Isn't that what they did to trace the location of a phone call? Could you trace a cellular or was that only a landline? Either way, the risk was too high. He'd never tell me anything anyway.

"Leave us alone," I said again and hung up.

"What did they want?" Scarlett asked.

"I'm not sure. But I'm thinking they might have been trying to trace my phone. We'd better go."

"Right." She frowned and skated with me toward the exit, clunking her feet along like a child who didn't get more candy. We turned in our skates and put on our shoes then headed for the lockers. When I glanced back at the rink, I saw two men on the bridge above, searching the crowd.

One of them turned, and his eyes fell directly on me. The one I called Deepthroat.

I shoved Scarlett behind me. "They're here. Put up your hood." How did they find us so fast? They must have known our general location before the phone call. Connor and Deepthroat split up, both sprinting for a different escalator.

I whipped my head around, looking for a place to hide. If we went back into the skate rental or across to the locker area, we'd be trapped. The elevator dinged behind us, and I grabbed Scarlett's hand and ran.

I pounded on the *door close* button. Two eons later, the elevator doors finally slid shut. But not before Connor saw us. He turned and headed back for the escalator, gesturing at Deepthroat to do the same.

When the doors opened on the second floor, I bolted for the nearest store, dragging Scarlett behind me. It was a large bookstore that took up the entire corner of the mall. We crouched down between a rack of magazines and shelves of giant coffee-table books.

"Did we lose them?" Her hand trembled as it clung to mine.

"I don't know."

Again, I wondered at the darkness she lived in. I shut my eyes for a second, trying to see the world from her point of view. When my lids closed, the objects that existed before still filled in the negative space. I could picture the cases of books and the plush reading chairs across the aisle.

My phone rang again, and I opened my eyes. Now was not the time for a foray into the world of blindness. I yanked out my phone. Deepthroat. I punched the decline icon. He insulted my intelligence. Did they really think I'd answer it again? Or were they listening for a ring-tone? I flipped the switch to mute, and a second later, the phone vibrated. This time the number was different but still unrecognized.

"They keep calling, trying to find us."

"Maybe that means we lost them," she said.

I released my grip on Scarlett and stood up slowly, just until I could peek over the racks of periodicals. Deepthroat paced the wide hallway outside the store, peering off in the opposite direction. I couldn't locate Connor.

"They're waiting outside the store," I whispered without turning around. "At least one is . . . not sure about the other." I craned my neck to see around the edge of the dark walnut bookcases. Did they split up again?

Scarlett gasped.

I spun around. Connor had her. One hand covered her mouth and the other squeezed her waist.

"Oldest trick in the book," he said. "Now, I'm taking the girl. You can let her go peacefully, or you can make a fuss and watch her die."

I thought *I* had a skewed sense of reality because of too much screen time, but this guy was off the charts. Was he really going to slit her throat right here in the middle of Barnes and Noble? Between *Newsweek* and *Great Castles of Britain*?

Scarlett fought his iron grip, but for him, it must have been like holding a cute, squirming kitten.

Without a second thought, I reached down, picked up a coffee-table book, and rammed it into his face with all my strength. I aimed for his jaw, looking for payback, but I missed. The book struck him across the nose, and I heard a little crack. Even better. He released Scarlett and staggered back a few steps. I didn't think he'd expected resistance.

I glanced at the book in my hand and, for the first time in my life, gained an appreciation for modern art. I tossed the book on the ground, grabbed Scarlett, and practically carried her out of the store, dashing out the side entrance. I heard someone ask, "Are you okay?" I assumed she was speaking to Connor, but I didn't turn around to find out.

The tall man lurked by the front entrance, still trying to lure us into a false sense of security by pretending to watch the wrong way. We ran across the hall into a discount clothing store.

This time, I wasn't going to hide and wait. My car was parked in the garage around the corner and down the main hall. But we were so easy to spot. A tall kid running through the mall, towing a very petite girl with pink hair. Even with the hood on, the pink was like a signal flare.

We moved to the back of the store and ended up by the dressing rooms. Some poor mom had abandoned her stroller there and hauled her kid in with her to try on clothes. It was one of those big, four-wheel-drive–type strollers.

"I have an idea." I yanked a blue casual dress shirt off a hanger and put it on over my T-shirt, tearing off the tags as discretely as possible. I tucked it in, hoping to look like a yuppie dad. I grabbed a baseball cap from another rack and jammed it on my head. I probably didn't need that. I had basically nondescript brown hair. I checked around to see if I'd been noticed, but the store was thankfully understaffed. Then I tiptoed over and wheeled away the stroller.

"Get in," I told her.

Scarlett took a step back and bumped into a rack of men's jackets. The hangers clanged, and a few pieces of clothing fell to the floor. "In what?"

I hefted her into the stroller.

"A pram?"

"Yeah, whatever." Even with her diminutive size, she was way too big. "Pull your legs up." If she could curl up behind the backseat of my car for twenty minutes undetected, she could hide in a stroller. A baby blanket lay wadded up in the storage basket underneath. I draped it over her then pulled the hood thing forward to conceal her as much as possible.

It wasn't exactly stealing, just borrowing. I guess the shirt and hat maybe, but the mom would get her stroller back eventually—when security found it abandoned in the parking garage. I could come back and pay for the clothes later if I lost sleep about it.

I pushed the stroller quickly, but hopefully calmly, out of the store. No sign of the Dynamic Duo. I pulled out my phone and pretended to talk while I pushed my large toddler down the passageways of the Lloyd Center Mall.

Out of the corner of my eye, I saw Connor and Deepthroat exit a store near the one we'd just left. Connor had a wad of napkins on his nose from the bookstore coffee shop. I grinned.

"I think they're behind us," I whispered to Scarlett. "But I'm not turning around to check." My palms were sweaty, and my heart raced.

"Come on, slowcoach," she said. "Get a wriggle on."

If two guys hadn't been hunting us through the mall, I would've asked what that could possibly mean. But we didn't have time right then for a language lesson. We'd reached the exit to the parking garage, and I wheeled her out through the glass double doors and into the garage elevator. I'd parked the car down on the lower level. When the doors closed and we were alone, I pulled back the stroller cover.

"We made it. I can't believe it worked," I said as my pulse began to stabilize.

"You know, I've never been in a pram before. It's kind of nice. I'll have to get me one." She laughed. "A little scary though. I might need my nappy changed." She chuckled at her little joke.

I wheeled her to the car and helped her out of the stroller. "Wait here while I go back for your clothes."

"No." She grasped at my arms. "You are not going back. And you are *not* leaving me here alone."

A group of gangly tweens walked past. "Hey," I called. "You guys want to make some money?"

They clustered together, casting me sidelong looks. But if there's one thing I'd learned growing up with a dead mother, it's that sympathy can be your friend. And so can money.

"Look, my girlfriend isn't feeling too great, and I can't leave her here alone because she's blind."

Scarlett made a point of staring off vacantly into space.

"I'll give you each five bucks if you get her stuff from our locker by the ice rink."

They huddled up and conferred for a few seconds, then one said, "Ten."

"Deal." I handed him the locker key. "There's two bags. And if you make it back in five minutes or less, I'll double it."

They took off running. I hated to think what their moms would say when they showed up with twenty bucks they got from a guy in the parking garage. Wasn't someone supposed to be teaching them not to talk to strangers?

Scarlett climbed into the passenger seat. I pushed the getaway stroller off to the side near a thick cement pillar then leaned back against my car and waited.

The boys came running back, breathing hard. But they beat the five-minute time limit. I loaded Scarlett's things into the back of the Rover then divvied out sixty dollars.

They mumbled thanks and trotted off, jabbering about their awesome luck.

I started the engine and looked at Scarlett. Her face was pale and drawn. She needed more help than I could give. I typed *Portland Police Department* into the Rover's navigation system.

CHAPTER SEVEN

CHRISTIAN VS. PROFESSIONAL HELP

I PULLED OUT OF THE parking garage. "Scarlett, I have something to tell you, and I want you to try to stay calm."

Bad choice of words. She bolted forward in her seat, but the seat belt caught and she slammed back. "What? What is it?"

"Calm," I reminded her. "Now, don't overreact, but I'm taking us to the cops."

She flung her arms out, one pressing against the window and the other restraining me. "No! It's not safe. They're all in on it together, the whole lot." She folded her arms across her chest with finality.

"I know that's what you said, but think about it. How can that be true?" She implied some kind of global kidnapping scheme involving the police in London and the Portland PD. "There's no way both sets of police are connected. You don't have proof that the London police had anything to do with your abduction. It has to be coincidence that you were taken right after going to them."

She didn't respond.

I put my hand on her shoulder. "Thing is, I'm out of my league with these guys." What could one kid really do against men like that? If I failed, I didn't lose the tennis match or get a bad grade on my report card; it was Scarlett's life. "I don't know how to keep you safe."

She took a deep breath, held it for a moment, and let it out with a huff. "All right. If you think it's the right thing to do." She turned her face away from me.

I headed to the nearest precinct, down by the riverfront. Three times they'd found us, and each time they'd gotten bolder. Connor had grabbed Scarlett right in the mall. I couldn't count on there always being a handy stroller nearby.

"Scarlett, what in the world is *get a wriggle on*? That sounds kind of . . . wrong."

She snorted despite the fact that she obviously tried not to. "It means hurry up."

"Of course it does." Where did she get all these crazy sayings? "I should've picked up a British-American dictionary while we were in the bookstore."

Another snort, this one slightly more relaxed than the first. "Speaking of, did you just take out Connor with your bare hands?"

Yeah. I was cool. "Actually, I hit him with *The Complete Guide to Modern Art, Volume 2.* I was going to use volume one, but I kind of like Picasso. So I went with two. I mean, who needs Jackson Pollock."

"I don't know. I've never seen either."

Stupid, stupid me. Just one more reason her life stank. "You're right. I'm sorry."

"Maybe you could show me sometime and describe them to me."

How could I describe something she'd never seen? Color, the texture of paint on canvas, the geometric arrangement of body parts in Picasso's cubism. "I'd love to."

I parked in front of the police station and helped Scarlett out of the car. She clumped along behind me, moving at a snail's pace. I told the man at the front desk that we wanted to report a crime. He gave me a clipboard full of tedious questions and told me to take a seat.

About ten minutes later, a different man came and escorted us to his desk. He was a few inches shorter than me, late thirties maybe, and had the beginnings of a gut that said time to lay off the donuts. Still, he looked like a guy you didn't mess with. The plaque on his desk identified him as Detective Scott Parker.

He scanned the clipboard and said, "You state here that two men assaulted you at a restaurant then followed you to a cabin at Hood River."

"Yes."

"Where was the restaurant?"

"Shari's, in Vancouver. Just off the 205." I didn't know the laws about out-of-state crimes, but Portland and Vancouver were basically the same city divided by the Columbia River. I hoped the bruise on my face and my cut lip might garner some support, so I mentioned the restaurant assault, even if it didn't mean anything in Oregon.

"And this happened yesterday?"

"Yeah. Well, they hit me in the restaurant yesterday; they broke into my cabin this morning. Then, just now, they chased us at the mall." Although I didn't have proof of any of it.

"*Your* cabin?" Interpretation: How does a seventeen-year-old kid own a cabin? Since no one besides me ever went there, I always referred to it as mine. "It's my mom's."

"Was she there?"

I wished he would just say what he meant. He fooled no one by asking all these questions with double meanings. What were two teenage kids doing alone at a cabin? Sex, alcohol, building a meth lab in the bathroom . . . everything I was morally opposed to.

Well, two could play at that game. I usually saved this card for later, but now seemed the right time. "My mother's dead."

Scarlett looked at me. Well, she didn't *look*, but her head flicked in my direction, and her mouth dropped open a little. With all the trouble of Scarface and Deepthroat, I hadn't spent much time giving her a replay of my own history.

Detective Parker stared at me then turned and clicked away at his keyboard. A minute or two later, he rose and went to a bank of printers lining the wall, returning with a photo printed on regular office paper. "Do you recognize this person?"

He held the picture in front of Scarlett. It was a testament to her abilities that people didn't catch on about her blindness right off the bat. I snatched the paper from Detective Parker's hand and gasped. "It's the waitress from Shari's." Why did he have a picture of her? I felt Scarlett stiffen beside me.

"I'm asking her," Parker said, tipping his head toward Scarlett.

"She's blind." Idiot. How many people wore sunglasses inside? Not really a fair accusation though, considering I'd been much slower on the uptake than him. "Why?" I asked.

Parker took the photo from me and set it on his desk. "She's dead. They found her body this morning a couple of blocks from the restaurant."

Scarlett's grip on my arm tightened. Dead? It had to be the work of Connor. My stomach dropped into my feet. These guys meant business. The waitress hadn't done anything. Why kill her? I rubbed my hand across my face.

"Says here"—he pointed to the computer screen in front of him, which I could only see the back of—"one witness came forward. He claims a teenage boy and a girl with pink hair came into the restaurant, made a big fuss about something, threatened the waitress, and then left."

Scarlett gripped my arm so hard her nails dug into my skin. She was right. Coming to the police was a huge mistake. The detective had essentially accused me of murder. Connor was always a step ahead. I'd bet anything he was the informant. Or his buddy, Deepthroat.

"Who was the witness? Did he have a scar across his eye?" I asked.

"That information is confidential."

Confidential? If he suspected me of killing someone, didn't I have a right to know my accuser? "Whoever it was is setting me up. I didn't do anything."

Detective Parker nodded in a way that suggested maybe I did and maybe I didn't; then he turned to Scarlett. "What's your story?"

I opened my mouth to answer, but the detective shook his head. "Let her speak."

"He didn't do it," she said. "He's telling the truth. Everything happened just like he said."

What? Why didn't she say anything about being kidnapped and stuffed in a suitcase or anything about her dreams? Especially if I was a suspect for murder. That could have been useful information in my defense. Did she seriously believe there was a big conspiracy and this guy was a dirty cop?

Parker leaned back in his chair and crossed his arms, studying Scarlett and me. "Why?"

"Why what?" I asked.

"Why'd he hit you, and why'd he follow you to the cabin?" He leaned forward and rested his elbows on his desk, clasping his hands. "Why are two guys—what was the word you used?" He glanced at the clipboard. "*Tracking* you, breaking into your mom's place without stealing anything, and chasing you through the Lloyd Center? And now you claim they're setting you up for murder?"

"Hey!" I pounded my fist on the desk and stood up. "I didn't kill anyone. Why would I walk in here asking for help if I was the murderer? They're lying. They're trying to cover their tracks and blame it on me." Some of the other cops glanced in our direction.

Detective Parker responded with a single raised eyebrow. I probably wasn't the first person to slam a fist on his desk.

"Sit down, sport. What about your dad?" he asked.

"What about him?" I sat, leaned back, and folded my arms.

"Why isn't he here, helping you? He's a big-shot lawyer."

How much information was on that glowing screen in front of him? "I don't live with him anymore. I moved out." Why did my voice have to crack when I said it? It'd been the best decision of my life, even if it hadn't worked out the way I'd planned.

"You ran away. That's what we call it when you're under eighteen. What'd he do? Beat you?"

I met his eyes and glared back. I hated his smugness. "No, he didn't beat me." *He ignored me.* Wasn't there a legal term for that? Child neglect or something? But how do you explain that when you have every material need and more? Besides, if he'd beaten me, that would have been acknowledging my existence.

Scarlett let out a long breath. "They're not after him. They're after me."

"Ah," he said, turning to Scarlett. "Now we're getting somewhere. You want to try again with your story?"

Scarlett tucked a strand of pink hair behind her ear and started with, "I was kidnapped—"

"Kidnapped. That's a pretty serious charge. Who kidnapped you?"

She waved her hand in front of her eyes. "Dunno, do I? I didn't get a good look at him."

Parker cringed. I wanted to high-five her for taking him down a notch.

"Was it Junior here?" he asked, pointing at me.

He wasn't as quick as I thought a police detective should be. I said to Scarlett, "He's pointing at me."

Parker realized he'd made another mistake, and I could see his mind working to process the pitfalls of communicating with someone who couldn't see. He clearly didn't like to be wrong.

"Course not. If it were him, why would he bring me here? No, it was one of the duffers from the restaurant, I think."

She related the account of her kidnapping from London, her escape, and then hiding in my car—kindly omitting the part where I left her on the highway. She still didn't mention her death dreams, and I guess I understood why. No one believed her in England, so why bring it up again here? She skimmed the truth by telling Parker her friend from school had gone missing and that she'd told the police. Then the kidnappers had come after her.

Parker asked for details of where she lived and which police station she'd reported it to in London. He listened and scribbled a few notes.

"So, let me see if I've got this straight." He leaned back in his chair again and clasped his hands behind his head. "You were kidnapped. But you're not here to press charges on the abduction." He turned to me and continued. "You came in to file a complaint about some guys who broke into your cabin and chased you in the Lloyd Center?"

"We came in here," I said, "because we want to be left alone. And didn't Scarlett just say one of them is the same guy?"

He nodded and typed on his keyboard again, and then he rose. "Okay. I'm going to have to keep you here for a while. Until we can get the death of the waitress sorted out."

"What? I'm under arrest?" *Unbelievable.* "This is crazy. I didn't do anything!"

"Then you don't need to worry. Empty your pockets."

I dumped my keys, wallet, and cell phone onto the desk. How could I not worry? I was being arrested for murder. I'd be eighteen in a few weeks; would I be tried as an adult? I swallowed hard. *Get a grip.* Don't fall apart here, not in front of the whole police department.

"You too," he told Scarlett.

She put her school ID card and a pack of bubble gum we'd bought in Hood River on the counter.

"Listen up," Detective Parker said. "You have the right to remain silent. Anything you say can and will be used against you in a court of law. You have the right to speak to an attorney. If you cannot afford an attorney," he cocked his head in a patronizing way, "one will be appointed to you. Do you understand these rights as they have been read to you?"

"Yeah, I got it."

"Morris, as a minor, you also have the right to have a parent present during questioning."

Great. That's just what I wanted. One more reason for my dad to look at me then look away disappointed.

"Becket, you're not a citizen of the United States, so you have the right to call your consulate before any questioning." In a softer voice, he added, "Do you understand what I've just explained to you?"

"Yes," she said. "I'm blind, not stupid."

Parker jerked his head back and glared. "Let's go."

"What about my phone call?" I'd have to call him now. Call my dad. There was no way around it. "I want my phone call," I yelled.

"Easy there, cowboy. You're not under arrest. I'm just holding you while I look this over, in case I have more questions." He cast me a slick grin. "I think you watch too much TV."

He herded us out a back door and down a hallway into a room where jail cells lined both sides. A solid cement wall separated the individual cells, and the fronts were steel bars. The first cage was full of gang-bangers all tatted up and wearing their pants below their bums. They cat-called at Scarlett as she passed. Across the aisle sat a man in a suit with his tie hanging loose around his neck, the dark circles below his eyes making his sockets look hollow.

The cell next to him was empty, and Detective Scott Parker waved us in like he was showing us to a room at a five-star hotel. When the door clanged shut, Scarlett jumped. At least he didn't separate us. I don't know what she would have done locked in a cell alone.

Parker walked away without a word.

Scarlett stood still, her face drained of color. Her cheeks had flushed with pink when we'd been ice-skating, and now they were the color of the ice.

I hugged her, holding her close and tight. "Hey, it's gonna be fine. We didn't do anything wrong." I had no idea what "detained for questioning" meant. Was I still a suspect?

Scarlett's body sagged. Once again, I'd blown it for her. I guess that was my life's purpose—to let everybody down. She deserved so much better.

The guys in the first cell were still jeering at us. I moved Scarlett to the back of the cell. We sat down on the bench sticking out of the wall, out of sight from the other inmates.

I put my arm around her. "Look on the bright side. At least we're safe from Connor in here."

She snorted. "I s'pose that's something."

"Seriously. Don't worry. We'll be out of here in no time." Although I wasn't sure how since I didn't get a phone call.

"In a chivvy," she said.

"What?"

"We'll be out of here in a chivvy."

Another Brit lesson. I gave her a weak laugh. "Sure, then. We'll be out of here in a chivvy."

She put her fingers on my face and touched it like she had the night before, when she wanted to *see* me. Was she looking for fear? I forced a smile, and her fingers lingered on my lips.

Did she not know what a turn-on that was? She tipped her head up, and I slipped her sunglasses off. Her eyes were red and tired. I couldn't concentrate with her fingers soft on my face like that. I pressed her sunglasses into her hand to give it something else to hold.

"Scarlett, I am so sorry. I feel like I'm making everything worse for you."

"Ha," she said with another sniff. "Thick as mince, aren't you? I'm the one ruining *your* life. Wouldn't be here locked up for murder if it weren't for me, would you? Wouldn't have gotten hit either, right?" She set her glasses on the bench beside her. "How old are you?"

"Almost eighteen."

"Why did you leave your dad?" She put her hand on my face again. It must be her way of watching people. How else could she sense the subtle changes in a person's countenance—expressions of sadness or joy. Or lies.

I tried to ignore how it made my breathing falter and my blood melt away. "My mom died when I was a kid, and my dad sort of checked out and never really checked back in. At least not into my life. I've lived with him all this time but totally alone. In his mind, I don't exist."

Nothing. That's what he'd called me. And that's what I was. "He remarried a year ago. Gloria. She just wants his money. I think he knows that but doesn't care. He works late every evening, comes home, drinks his expensive wine, then goes to bed. Months will pass without a word to me. Without even a look."

Scarlett took her hand off my face and leaned against the wall. "All parents are berks."

Another word I didn't know, but judging by the venom in her voice, I agreed. She closed her eyes and let her head fall against my arm.

According to the Miranda, I had the right to a parent and a lawyer. In my case, they were one and the same. I dreaded that phone call—if they ever let me make it. But I still couldn't quite figure out my dad in all of this. Why did he call me after I left? What was the point in taking up pretense now, when he could've at last been rid of me?

I think Scarlett dozed off. We'd been sitting there over an hour, freezing our fannies off on the cold metal bench, when Detective Parker came back.

"Morris, someone's here for you. You're free to go."

"What about Scarlett?"

The detective cast a questioning look down the hall to someone I couldn't see. What if it was Connor and Deepthroat? Here to bail us out of the frying pan and into the fire? I went to the front of the cell and followed Parker's gaze.

"Who is it?" Scarlett asked.

I gripped the cold, steel bars. "It's my dad."

CHAPTER EIGHT
CHRISTIAN VS. THE ICE MAN

My father stood in the entrance to the jail room, wearing his usual dark gray suit. Our eyes met, and he looked at me for the first time in a long time. The air whooshed out of me like when I backed my car over a basketball. There was nothing left but a limp hide covering an empty, concave shell.

"Sir?" Detective Parker asked my dad. No wonder I didn't get my phone call. Apparently, Parker had made it for me.

My father gave him a nod and walked away. Was he mad? Disappointed? Indifferent? I couldn't tell. He always wore the same infuriating, expressionless mask.

"You can both go," Parker said.

I went back for Scarlett. She put her glasses on and followed me out. Parker handed me a manila envelope labeled *Christian Morris/Personal Effects*. He had a similar one for Scarlett, only smaller and very thin. He held it out to her.

I took the envelope from him and touched it to her hand. "Here's your stuff," I said.

My dad waited in the lobby of the police station. "You ready, then?" he asked when I stood in front of him.

"Yeah," I said, not sure what else to say.

Scarlett cleared her throat.

"Oh, um. This is Scarlett. Scarlett, Richard Morris."

My dad reached out a hand. "Nice to meet you," he said.

Scarlett didn't respond. I lifted Scarlett's hand into his, and they gave a quick shake. His mask faltered, and he looked at me with surprise. I caught a glimpse of something else too, but it was gone before I could identify it. We walked to our cars in silence. He'd parked next to me.

* * *

"Where's Gloria?" I asked when we entered an empty house. Scarlett hung on one arm, and I carried her bags of new clothes in the other.

"I sent her to Vegas with her mother for the weekend."

No regrets on my part. Maybe she'd strike it rich on roulette and never come back.

I was halfway up the stairs with Scarlett when my dad said, "Christian, after you take her to her room, you'll come see me in my study."

He turned away before I had a chance to answer. He'd never demanded a one-on-one before. This didn't bode well. Not that I had a choice; he'd just bailed Scarlett and me out of jail.

Our house had four large bedrooms on the upper level, each with its own bathroom. Mine was in the northeast corner, where I had views of the city and the rose gardens to the east and the West Hills to the north. At one time, a nanny had occupied one of the bedrooms. She had stayed with us for a few years, cooking and tending. Then Dad let her go. Another painful memory I wished I didn't have: I had won Best in Class for a drawing I did in ninth-grade art, and they were displaying it at some stupid afterschool art show for all of the kids and their parents. Nanny Mavis plucked up her courage and suggested to my father that he should go. He refused, dismissing my existence by using the *nothing* word again, and told her she had one week to find another post. That was the last time I'd had anything resembling a parent.

I led Scarlett to the nanny's empty room. I showed her around, guiding her to the bathroom and setting her bags out so she could unload them. She took off her jacket and laid it across the plush reading chair in the corner. She set her sunglasses on the dresser, feeling and touching everything as she moved through the room.

"Is there anything else you need?" I asked, hoping she'd need something that took a really long time—like a road trip to Miami. I'd rather do more clothes shopping than face my dad in his study.

"Food," she said.

Of course. It'd been at least nine hours since we'd had a drive-thru breakfast-slash-lunch on the way back from Hood River. "Do you like pizza?" I asked. Tomorrow I'd have to add some fruits and vegetables to our diet before we died from carb overload.

"Love it."

I pulled out my phone and sat on the bed, texting in a pizza order to the restaurant a few blocks away. "It'll be here in about twenty minutes. Is that okay?"

"Brill." She plopped down on the bed next to me.

I laughed, even though my nerves were at the breaking point. Suspected of murder and my dad waiting for me downstairs. I wasn't sure which was worse. And then there was Scarlett. Not that I put her in the same category as murder and lousy fathers. Not by a long shot. But what was I supposed to do with her and all her pink hair and diamond nose stud and nonsensical British idioms? "You know, half the time, I don't really know what you're saying."

She reached up and put her hands on my face then kissed my cheek in a slow, deliberate way. "Do you know what I'm saying now?"

I turned to look at her, my face inches from hers. I lived in a desert, completely parched and withered from lack of affection. I'd had girls interested in me before, but they'd always seemed more excited about my money than my actual self. Scarlett's gentle touch, her lips on my cheek, they were different. The floodgate opened, and I soaked it up, thirsting for more. I leaned down and kissed her. She moved into me, her mouth soft and warm on mine.

I was exhausted from the day, and my guard was down. I didn't trust myself, so I pulled away. "Scarlett, I don't think this is a good idea." I searched her eyes, looking for an emotion to let me know how she felt. They didn't show anything, just a blank wall of velvet brown.

She sighed and leaned back. "Sorry. I guess that wasn't fair." She sounded upset. Or maybe hurt. Her feelings were so hard to read. I'd seen Scarlett frown and smile, and her chin quivered when she cried. But she didn't reveal any emotions through her eyes.

I lifted her hand to my face, hoping that would help her know I meant what I was going to say. "Not because I don't want to, but I just can't right now. My dad's waiting for me, and I should go get that over with."

"Right."

"I'll come get you when the pizza's here." I glanced around her room. What could I give her to do while she was alone? My books and magazines were worthless. The TV? "Um, do you want some music or something?"

"No. I'll just unpack and stuff. You best be off."

I started for the door, but she called me back.

"Yes?"

"Thanks for the best day ever."

I raised my eyebrows and remembered for the hundredth time that that was pointless. "If starting the day hiding in a garbage can and ending it in jail is the best day you've ever had, your life is worse than I thought."

I turned and lumbered down the stairs, dragging my feet over the slate tiles of the main hall toward my dad's study.

The door was closed. I stared at the knotty grain in the wood. I hadn't been in his sanctuary for over a year. After I'd turned sixteen, I'd summoned all my courage to knock on this door and ask if I could borrow his car to take a girl to junior prom. He was reading some notes on a yellow legal pad. Without glancing up, he fished the keys out of his pocket and tossed them to me. "Not a scratch," he said.

The next day he came home with the Range Rover. "Here's your own car." *Interpretation: Now you can leave me alone.*

That was the last time we'd spoken—until now, when he'd summoned me to his study. If only we were closer to Mount Hood. Then, with any luck, some boiling lava from the volcano would bubble up through the floor and swallow me.

I clenched my fists and knocked twice with my knuckles.

"Enter."

He'd taken off his suit coat and draped it over the back of his leather desk chair. His room was spotless, not even a stray sticky note to show he ever used it. Black and white photos of glacial mountains, all snow and jagged rocks, hung on the wall above his head. On the opposite side, in shelves of wrought iron and steel, rested volumes of legal books.

I noticed for the first time that his black hair had steely-gray flecks around the temples. I got my height and solid build from my dad. The rest of my looks came from Mom. The brown hair, blue eyes. He motioned for me to sit in a chair across the desk from him. It was like I was back in the police station with Detective Parker. Only the police station felt friendlier.

I lowered myself down onto the shiny metal chair frame and black sparsely-padded seat cushion. I folded my arms and examined my shoes. My cool, expensive shoes that all the kids in my high school wished they had. I owned a pair in every color.

"Why did you leave?" he asked.

That was his first question? He was a brilliant man who made his living by dragging the truth out of the hardest of criminals. He must have already known the answer. How could he treat me like this for eight years and then not have a clue why I left? Anyway, how was the motive behind my running away more interesting than *why were you in jail for murder?*

I shrugged, concentrating all my efforts on keeping my face impassive. "I'll be eighteen in two months. I thought it would be better to leave at the beginning of the school year instead of partway through." For years,

I'd planned that the moment I was legal, I'd be gone. Last week, I moved plans forward a few months.

That answer didn't fully explain the *why*. But since I wasn't under oath, I felt no need to divulge more than absolutely necessary. If I wanted to maintain any level of composure, I couldn't think about the real reason—the one sitting on the other side of the desk.

I lifted my gaze from my stylish feet and found him staring at me, his lawyer eyes drilling into me.

"Tell me about the girl."

I started with the same story I told Connor in the restaurant. "I found her on the side of the road. She was alone. I took her to Shari's for a meal. While we were there, some guys came in looking for trouble. We left, and the next morning the waitress was found dead. The guys in the restaurant told the police I killed her. We went to the police because those thugs were still harassing us, and the detective slammed us in jail."

It was the bare-bones truth, and I kept steady eyes on my dad. Already, this was the longest conversation I could remember having with him in my entire life. I cursed the beads of sweat betraying me on my forehead and the way my throat kept getting tighter and tighter.

"Where is she from?"

"London." This was really beginning to feel like the courtroom.

"Why is she here alone?"

I looked back at my shoes. He knew how to ask the important questions. The ones that cut to the core without wasting time on the periphery.

Should I tell him she was kidnapped? Scarlett seemed hesitant to bring that up. I could lie. Even if he knew I was lying, I doubted he'd do anything about it. But I didn't want to lie. Regardless of all the emptiness between us, he was my dad. I wanted to tell him the truth. I wanted him to know that killers were chasing me, that I cared about the girl upstairs. That my life was so chock full of misery, I'd ended up on the bathroom floor.

Then he finds me in jail. Isn't that when dads are supposed to ask questions like *Are you okay? Do you need help?* Not my dad. He wanted to know about the girl.

Why couldn't he see me? What was so wrong with me that he didn't care about me at all? *Come on, lava.* There had to be some magma churning under Portland; we weren't that far from the volcano. *Boil up and save me.*

I blinked hard, working my jaw to get back in control. "She doesn't have a family." I lost it on the last word and had to grit my teeth to steady my voice. Who even knew what a family was anymore? Not me. I steeled myself before meeting his gaze. He seemed not to notice that his son was falling apart. He must've seen it in the courtroom every day.

The doorbell rang, and I stood up. "I ordered a pizza. We haven't eaten in a long time, and Scarlett gets hungry."

He walked around the desk and held my chin with one hand, tilting my head to get a better view of Connor's handiwork. His hand was warm and gentler than I'd expected. It wasn't the father's touch I longed for, but it was so much better than the nothing.

I ached for that hand to pat me on the back, to give me an awkward, father-to-grown-up-son hug, a squeeze on the shoulder. Anything. Anything to indicate he cared more about me than he did about the icy mountain peaks framed behind him.

"Thanks for coming for me," I whispered.

He dropped his hand and said in a cold, steady tone, "If you run away again, I'll cut you off from everything. Do you understand?"

I nodded, and he strode out of the den. I watched him walk down the hall until he disappeared into his bedroom. His shoulders slumped as he moved out of sight.

A prisoner again. Why did he care whether I stayed in his house or not? Did he want the control? Or was it the money? Was he mad about what I'd taken from his safe? He didn't sound mad. He sounded . . . disappointed.

The doorbell rang again, followed by a loud knock. The pizza.

I went in the opposite direction of my father and swung open the heavy front door. I paid the guy, put the food on the kitchen counter, and went up for Scarlett.

She lay on her back, spread eagle. "Comfy bed. How'd it go with your father?"

"Fine."

"Was he mad?"

"No. He's never mad," I said, my voice raw and scratchy.

"You sound like you've been in the wars."

"I guess I kind of feel like it. Pizza's here. You hungry or not?" Maybe I just needed some food too. Something to get my blood sugar up and my head thinking clearly.

"All right, all right. Don't get yer knickers in a twist." She scooted off the bed and held out her hand.

I shook my head. "Okay, now you're just doing it on purpose."

"What?"

"Spouting random phrases that you know I'll never understand."

"Well, knickers are—"

"No. Don't explain. I got that one."

I led Scarlett to the kitchen and found my dad rummaging through the fridge. He had a wineglass on the counter filled with burgundy liquid. If I'd been alone, I'd have turned and walked away. Especially tonight, after the interrogation. But Scarlett was hungry. I sat her in the center of the kitchen at the island bar.

"Hi, Mr. Morris. Want some pizza?" she said out of nowhere.

All activity in the kitchen ceased. Dad was reaching for his drink— no doubt working on his own getaway—when his hand froze. My plates halted halfway to the counter. A perfectly innocent smile played on Scarlett's face, like an angel with a halo of pink. She didn't wear her dark glasses. I think she knew I preferred her eyes without the barrier.

I didn't dare look up. I'd seen enough of him for one day. I just carried on like we always did, pretending the other didn't exist. I put a slice on a plate and set it front of Scarlett. I placed her hand on the crust edge and said, "Meat Lover Madness. I hope you're hungry."

"Starved."

I put a soda in her other hand. She sipped it then set it down. "Disgusting. What is that?"

Dad leaned back against the counter, watching. My appetite was quickly slipping away, replaced by coils of rope that knotted themselves tighter and tighter the longer he stayed.

"It's root beer," my father said.

I almost dropped my food on the floor.

"Never heard of it." She took another sip and shuddered. "Nasty. And so sweet. Tastes like cough syrup."

In some ways, Scarlett wasn't too far off. But when my mom was alive, we used to have pizza night on Fridays, and she always served it with root beer.

"It's the best drink when you're having pizza," Dad said, taking a plate from the cupboard and sliding a slice onto it.

The tip of my pizza drooped, stalled between the plate and my open mouth. A pepperoni slithered toward the edge. Was he eating with us? And chatting? He wouldn't look at me, but still, this was unprecedented.

He picked up his glass of wine and dumped it down the drain, feeding the sewers about a hundred dollars' worth of Bordeaux. He twisted a plastic bottle of root beer out of the six-pack. "I'll just . . . leave you two alone now."

"Thanks again, Mr. Morris," Scarlett said. "For everything."

My dad nodded at her then left the room, meeting my eyes for a split second as he passed. The pepperoni slid off my pizza and slapped onto the floor. Strings of mozzarella dangled after it, reaching out to bring it home.

Scarlett tried to pull another slice from the box. I'd been so distracted by my dad's strange behavior, I hadn't noticed her groping for the pizza container.

"Here, let me get that." I put two more slices on her plate and cleaned up the lost pepperoni. What was he up to? Just being polite to a guest? It's true he wasn't the Ice King to everyone. Other people really liked him. He was a huge success at work and one of the best lawyers in the city. He must have some good qualities; he just never shared them with me.

Scarlett and I ate and talked and laughed for a while then went up to turn in. It was almost midnight, and the strain of the day had pushed me over the edge. I showed Scarlett my room down the hall in case she needed anything during the night then crawled into bed.

I dreamed we were eating at Shari's restaurant. When the waitress asked us for our order, her neck was slit open and blood stained her clothing. Scarlett screamed like a demon possessed. I bolted out of bed.

I heard the scream again; it came from Scarlett's room.

Dream or bad guys? Hard to tell. What if Connor had found her? If he found us at the cabin, he'd have no trouble tracking us here. But we had a security system, and we weren't alone. I grabbed a tennis racket—it was all I had—and raced down the hall. She screamed again.

CHAPTER NINE

CHRISTIAN VS. THE NIGHTMARE

I BURST INTO SCARLETT'S ROOM, tennis racket cocked and ready. She tossed and turned in her bed, moaning and crying. Other than Scarlett, the room was empty. Another dream. Did she have them every night?

"Scarlett, wake up." I shook her gently. "Hey, it's just a dream, wake up."

She stopped thrashing, and her eyes popped open. She sat up and asked, "Where's Christian?"

"I'm right here. I think you're having a nightmare."

She sat still for minute, her panting gradually subsiding. "I had another dream." She leaned her head on my chest.

I stroked her short hair and rubbed her back like I'd seen loving parents do on television. "Was it Katie again?"

She shook her head. "No. It was someone else." Her voice was softer than a whisper but also strained and sore.

Did that mean she was predicting the death of another person? "Who was it? Do you want to tell me about it?"

Again, she shook her head.

Something creaked in the hall downstairs, like the sound of a person sneaking. "Quiet. There's someone in the house." I didn't need to say it; she'd heard it too.

I tried to rise, but she tightened her grip on my shirt. "Don't go. They'll kill you."

I pressed a finger to my lips. Idiot. Would I never learn? "Shh." I pried her hand off my shirt and crept toward the door, holding the tennis racket at the perfect angle so that when I smacked the intruder, it would be with the rim and not the sweet spot.

Dim light from the street lamps shone in through the big window in the entryway and cast a long shadow that crept toward Scarlett's room. I jumped out, yelling like a barbarian.

My dad stood in the hallway, both hands holding a heavy black handgun pointed at my chest. Instantly, his hands dropped to his sides. "Christian," he said breathlessly. "You startled me."

"You have a gun?" How did I not know that? Just because we never talked didn't mean I wasn't good at snooping. I thought I knew everything about his possessions, but this really surprised me.

"I heard screams. Is everything okay?"

"Yeah. Scarlett has nightmares. I went in to check on her." I couldn't take my eyes off his weapon. "Why do you have a gun?"

"Why do you have a tennis racket?"

Did I detect sarcasm in his voice? "In case there's a bad guy," I said.

"Exactly." He turned and went down the stairs, back to his room.

Did he just joke with me?

I glanced down at the racket by my side and realized I was wearing a T-shirt and boxers. I thought I should put pants on before going back to Scarlett. Then I remembered it didn't matter. *Put some on anyway*, I told myself.

"Was it your dad?" she asked from two feet behind me.

I jumped so high I nearly hit the ceiling. "Okay, everyone in this house needs to stop sneaking around." I took Scarlett's arm. "You. Back to bed."

She slipped under her covers. With any luck, she'd make it through the rest of the night without dreaming. I shuffled back to my bedroom, tossing the racket in the closet as I passed. Even though the incident was over now, I pulled on some sweat pants anyway before hopping back in bed.

I lay in the dark, eyes wide, listening to my heart rate slow. I pictured men creeping around outside the house, women with long hair pulled up in a knot performing surgery, a dead waitress lying in the rhododendrons on the other side of the river, my dad with his hand on my chin.

"Are you awake?" It was an almost inaudible whisper at my door.

"Yes."

Scarlett pushed the door open the rest of the way and tiptoed in. "Where are you?"

"I'm over here."

She followed my voice until she bumped into my bed. "I'm scared."

I sat up and flipped on my lamp.

For the first time, I saw something in her eyes. Behind that wall of milk-chocolate brown, she was terrified.

"Hey, hey, hey," I said, pulling her onto the bed beside me. "You don't have to be scared. You're safe here. This house has an excellent alarm system, and no one can get in without detection."

"Then why were you carrying a tennis racket?" She let out a laugh that she obviously didn't feel. "Anyway, that's not why I'm scared. I don't want to go back to sleep."

Who could blame her? Who wants to dream of people dying and then wake up only to have it all come true? "What happened in your dream? Who did you see?"

"Christian, I was wrong about my first dream. It wasn't Katie on the operating table." She broke into a sob. "It was me."

No way. It couldn't be. She wasn't with them anymore. She was with me. How could she still dream about her own death when she was away from the killers? Maybe the dreams weren't really a prediction of the future. Maybe what happened with her grandma was just a fluke. And the landlord. And his wife. And perhaps others she'd never mentioned. "Are you sure? If you were wrong before, maybe you're wrong again."

"I'm sure. I didn't recognize myself the first time. But now I know. I dreamed it again tonight. It's me." Her little body shuddered, and her tears left dark spots on my navy-blue duvet. What could I say? How do you comfort a person who has just seen her own death?

"Listen," I said. "We can change it. We already have. You got away from them. You're safe here."

She said nothing, just rocked back and forth.

"You've had the dream twice, right?"

"Yes." She sniffed.

"And it still hasn't happened. That's because it won't. We fixed it. Your subconscious mind just doesn't know how to process that. So it sent the dream again." That made sense. I'd almost convinced myself.

She nodded.

"What about Katie?" I asked. If she wasn't the girl in the dream, maybe she was safe and sound back in England. "Is she still in danger?"

"She was in my dream, alive. She was in the surgery with us, helping."

One thing I'd learned about Scarlett in our short time together was that when the truth was hard to swallow, she had a great knack for keeping it out of her mouth. "Helping you? Or helping them?"

"Helping them." She cried hard now. Her whole face was wet with tears. I went to my bathroom and brought her a roll of toilet paper. She unrolled a few squares and dabbed at the mess.

"Let's get you back to bed. In the morning, we'll figure something out, okay?"

"Sure."

"How would you say, 'Don't give up?'"

She snorted then quickly wiped her nose. "Don't lose your bottle."

"Don't lose your bottle? That sounds more like something you'd say to the town drunk."

She laughed halfheartedly, but the fear in her eyes dissolved, and their color went back to vacant brown.

I escorted her back to her bedroom and stood at the door for a few minutes. "I'll wait here until you fall asleep, okay?"

"You can sit in the chair," she offered hopefully. She really didn't want to be alone.

"Boundaries. Remember?"

"Right. The gentleman." She rolled onto her side and lay still.

Those dreams must really drain her because it didn't take long until her breathing organized itself into slow, steady breaths. I tiptoed back to bed and let myself relax, finding at last the sleep my body had been craving.

* * *

"'Bout time," she said when I walked into the kitchen the next morning, yawning and still in my sweats.

"Why, what time is it?" I asked as I glanced at the clock on the microwave.

"Dunno, do I? No talking clocks here, eh." She sat on a bar stool and was showered and dressed in another new outfit of varying shades of black. I guess that made it easier to match.

No wonder she went for color in her hair. Who was responsible for the shocking pink though? Did someone say, *Scarlett, your wardrobe is bland. Why not color the front sections of your hair something fluorescent?*

"Why is your hair pink? You keep telling me you don't know colors. Who picked pink?"

"I did." She sounded proud of herself. "My gran used to give me bubble gum. I could blow huge bubbles with it. Bubble gum isn't so easy to get in the UK, mind, so it was a real treat. She told me a million times to keep that pink gum out of my hair."

"So you put it in permanently. I guess that's kind of cool."

"Yeah, well, the dentist told me not to chew sugary gum, didn't he? Bad for my teeth. Now get moving. I'm fantastically bored. And hungry."

"It's Saturday, and I'm seventeen. I'm supposed to sleep till noon. It's only ten thirty." But I went back up to shower and get dressed anyway.

After a breakfast of french toast—which she loved, but not the syrup, too sweet—we called her guy-friend in England again. Still no answer. I wanted Scarlett to be safe, but part of me cheered up knowing she'd be with me a little longer.

I set my laptop up on the kitchen counter. I wanted to see if I could find any more information on the deceased waitress and get answers to some of the other questions that circulated in the back of my mind.

I pulled up the *Columbian*, the newspaper for Vancouver. There was a short article in yesterday's news, but it didn't tell me more about the waitress than the detective had. I Googled "how to trace the location of someone using a cell phone." It turned out to be pretty easy, and anyone could do it. *Note to self: When leaving the house, turn power completely off.*

I read everything out loud to Scarlett. She listened with interest, and it hit me again how different her world was from mine. She couldn't read a computer screen or even tell the time. Things I did a thousand times a day without a second thought. Yet she navigated through the darkness so well that it was easy to forget she couldn't see.

I decided to take Scarlett to the cemetery to see if she could find her way back to the building she had escaped from, or at least point us in the right direction. I had stopped there on my way out in the late afternoon. Did she walk all night and into the day or hide most of the time, listening and waiting? If we could find something close by, maybe we'd be able to tell the police and get Deepthroat off our backs and clear my murder allegations.

I also found the name of a little store downtown that sold special aids for the vision impaired. I didn't know how long Scarlett would be here, but she ought to at least be able to know the time and use the computer. According to the meager website, they carried talking watches and clocks, computer software for screen readers, and some Braille books.

Cemetery first. We drove the short distance up to West Hills Memorial Gardens. On the south end of the cemetery sat a big, rundown mortuary, and the old-growth trees of Forest Park bordered the rest. A light rain fell from dreary gray skies—typical Portland weather. I decided maybe I should rethink my first plan of moving to Canada and find somewhere south to finish up my senior year. Somewhere with sun and sand.

I drove straight to my mother's grave and parked the car by the big cedar tree. Scarlett waited for me to come around and get her. She looked so tiny again, standing by the car in the rain. I pulled her in close, under the umbrella.

She hooked her hand into the crook of my arm, and we walked among the rows of headstones, our feet mushing in unison in the damp grass, the smell of wet pine heavy in the air. Somewhere along the way, I slid my arm down until I held her hand, our fingers laced.

"This is my mom's grave," I told her. A big, flat slab of stone stood about a foot off the ground. Simple but stately.

She crouched down and ran her fingers over the polished granite, reading the words as she went. "Catherine Cooper Morris. That's a nice name. What was she like?"

"I don't remember her much. It was a long time ago, and I was young."

"C'mon. I told you about Gran, didn't I? Let's hear it."

"Well." I poked around into the depths of my memories. "She loved the cabin at Hood River." I hadn't talked about my mother to anyone for a long time. Not because it was painful but because my memories were so vague. Just a few simple moments that came to me like a three-second video clip.

"We went there almost every weekend during the summer," I said. "She was fascinated by Mount Hood. My dad didn't work so much then. He was with us on Saturdays and Sundays. He would build a roaring fire, Mom would make popcorn, and we'd sit on the couch and watch a movie. I would wedge myself in between them, and they'd think they were so sneaky, kissing over my head. I always fell asleep before the end."

Scarlett stood up and wiped her damp hand on her jacket. Well, my jacket. "A perfect life."

"I guess. Anyway, about eight years ago she got sick and died."

"What happened to your dad?"

"I don't know. He just never really looked at me again." Why did that hurt so much more than the loss of my mother? When my mom passed away, I thought my life was over. I was right, but not for the reasons I'd expected. I'd recovered from Mom's death. My own death in my father's eyes tormented me daily.

Scarlett slipped her hand back into mine. "What did you do?"

"I cried, when I was younger. Then I turned into a terror, causing trouble at home and at school. When that didn't get Dad's attention, I turned to drugs. He never seemed to notice when I came home smelling like cigarette smoke—or worse. I'm not sure he even knew. I only caught sight of him a few times a month at most." That was when Jay came along, scraping me off the bench and shoving me back into the game.

"I finally decided that nothing could reach Dad, so I gave up. I studied hard, got good grades, and figured my only hope was to get into a decent college as far away from him as possible. Make a new life, without a family."

"Why did you run away on the day we met? You said you had to finish your last year of high school. So why leave early?"

She'd been honest with me about her miserable life, so I told her the cold, hard truth. My low point. My shame. "I tried to kill myself."

"Crikey O'Reilly!"

"Yep. I took a bunch of pills and woke up hours later in a pile of my own vomit. How's that for a nice anecdote? He never knew. I thought if I died he might finally care.

"That's when I knew I had to get out before the end of the year. Before my powers of judgment failed me again. Three days later, I found you in the back of my car."

She lifted both hands to my face, seeing with her fingers the furrow in my brow and the tight line of my lips. "Berks, like I said."

"Berks?"

"Gits. Idiots. Parents."

"Oh, right."

Her touch lingered on my mouth. I think she did it on purpose this time, knowing how irresistible it was. I leaned down and kissed her, pressing her against me and lifting her body off the ground until she stood on my mother's gravestone, equalizing our height.

"Scarlett?" I said.

"Yeah?"

"You're the most interesting, amazing, and beautiful girl I've ever met."

"What?"

"I just want you to hear the truth about yourself, in case no one has ever told you." I brushed a lock of damp hair from her face. "I know what it's like to be deserted by a parent, always wondering what you've done wrong to never deserve their love. You shouldn't have to feel that way."

She smiled. "Now you're just taking the Mickey."

I laughed out loud. "I swear you're making these up."

"I'm not. Honest. My gran watched a lot of telly. I picked up only the best of the Queen's English. It means you're teasing."

"Well, I'm not giving you Mickey. I'm serious."

She snorted. "*Taking* the Mickey. If you can't get it right, don't even try."

She pulled me in for another kiss. I dropped the umbrella on the grass so I could give Scarlett's lips my full attention.

CHAPTER TEN

CHRISTIAN VS. THE RECEPTIONIST

SCARLETT WASN'T SURE WHICH DIRECTION she'd come from to get to the cemetery. I tried to get details. How big was the tree? Did she smell flowers? How long did it take her?

All she knew for sure was that she'd walked until she'd felt warmth from the sun. Then, worried she might be spotted, she hid in the bushes. She must've stayed there for hours, frozen from wandering all night in the cold and wet, wearing only her *Mind the Gap* T-shirt. Not to mention the stress of never knowing for sure if she was fully concealed or not.

When she'd heard me pull in and the car door open and close, she waited a few minutes then slunk over and quietly climbed in. Not much to go on.

We sloshed back to the Rover and cruised the surrounding roads, me searching for some kind of medical-looking facility, Scarlett basking in the warmth of her seat heater. I didn't see anything promising. A couple of rich people's houses, and that was all.

Most of the area surrounding the cemetery was Forest Park. Plenty of druggies hung out there, the backdrop of the occasional murder or rape that showed up in the news. It was a miracle she'd made it to the cemetery in the middle of the night alone. She must've been terrified. And then, when she thought she was safe, some moron had dumped her on the highway. I groaned out loud just thinking about it.

"What's wrong?" she asked with her eyes still closed.

"Nothing. I was just thinking."

"About what?" She turned her face to me.

"About what a loser I am."

She laughed. "There's still time. Football is a game of two halves."

First of all, football has four quarters and has nothing to do with my mental state. I opened my mouth to ask for interpretation, but she cut me off. "Nope. I'll let you figure that one out."

* * *

The store for the vision and hearing impaired was near the complex of facilities surrounding the university's medical center. I parked out front of the run-down building in one of the few spaces not labeled *handicapped*. Two giant fir trees shaded the parking lot from the sun that was making a feeble attempt to break through the clouds and drizzly rain.

"Can I help you find something?" an older man behind the counter asked. He had silver hair and thick, square glasses.

"Yeah. We're looking for . . . a clock?" All kinds of contraptions—special telephones, red-tipped canes, flashing doorbells, and huge Braille machines—lined the walls and filled the rickety shelves. I didn't know half this stuff existed. "What do you want, Scarlett?"

She pulled me aside. "I don't need anything. I'm fine. You've spent too much on me already."

"If you're going to be here a few days, you need some things to make it easier. Really, it's okay."

"Won't your dad get mad?"

"I told you. He never gets mad. He won't even know." But that made it sound like we were sneaking around behind his back. "What I mean is, he doesn't care enough to pay attention. I spend his money all the time, and he never says a word. Besides, he likes you." What else could explain his strange behavior last night?

She didn't answer.

"A watch," I told the old man. "Do you have something that tells the time out loud?"

He led us to a glass case filled with watches. "Most people don't want a talking watch. They like Braille. Quieter. Do you read Braille?" he asked Scarlett.

"Yes."

"A talking watch is for people who've recently lost their vision. They can't read Braille too well. No one wants to check the time in the middle of church and announce to everyone there's still half an hour to sit through, if you know what I mean."

I did know what he meant. His point made sense. A watch that told the time to everyone in hearing distance broadcasted *blind person*. Scarlett didn't seem like the kind of girl who would want that.

She remained silent. Reluctant, I assumed, to let me spend more money on her.

"Let's look at that one." I pointed to a watch with a thick black leather band and a silver face. It looked like something Scarlett would wear—it matched her boots.

"That's a men's watch." He pointed to the other half of the display case where delicate, gold-banded watches or shiny silver ones sat in neat rows. "These are the women's."

"Bring out that gold one." I pointed down. "And the men's one. We'll let Scarlett choose."

He set them on the counter, and I put one in each of her hands. "What do you think?" I asked. It took her half a second to choose the black one. I smiled.

The man packaged it up and asked if we needed anything else. With a lot of persuasion, I convinced her to choose a book as well. I read her a bunch of titles, but in the end, she made me do the picking.

"Here," I said, pulling one off the shelf and handing it to her. "It's about a girl who falls in love with a vampire. All the chicks at school are in love with it." The book cost almost as much as the watch. I could see why such a thing was a rarity for her.

The old man took his time ringing up the items, cataloging each one in an old ledger book before typing the price into a stone-age computer. I browsed the myriad pamphlets stacked on the counter that advertised everything from human sight-guides for hire to experimental eye treatments that could restore vision.

I picked up a few and thumbed through them. One caught my eye. On the cover, the words *Sight for the Blind* were printed in bold, clear letters, and under that, a picture of an attractive woman in a lab coat, with long hair pulled up in a bun, and wearing glasses.

Inside, it talked about a new silicon retinal microchip that could be surgically implanted to cure blindness.

"What's this?" I asked the man.

"That," he said with a touch of awe, "is Dr. Anne Wyden. She's built a tiny computer chip that goes right in the eye. Sends images to the brain."

"Does it work? Can it make a blind person see?" This would be perfect. What if we could get the procedure for Scarlett? I'd have to talk to my dad about it, but it'd be worth it if she could see.

"Someday, it's going to change lives," he said. "Right now, it might make it so you don't bump into the furniture. Look on the back."

I flipped it over and saw a series of pictures. The first showed a room with a couch, plant, and table lamp in normal vision. An average living room. The second showed the same scene with the use of the retinal chip. It was like looking at a black and white monitor with a resolution of four pixels per square inch. You could barely identify the objects. I guess if your choice was that or nothing, four pixels was better. I'd anticipated something a lot more sophisticated.

"She's a brilliant doctor," the old man continued. "And she takes on a lot of charity cases. Every year she offers the procedure to five people who could otherwise never afford it. But it won't help everyone." He handed me the bag of Scarlett's stuff. "It only works on degenerative eye conditions; that's what most of my customers have. Her clinic is just up the road. You could make a visit."

"Thanks." I took the pamphlet, and we left.

In the car, I helped Scarlett put on her new watch. She kept lifting the glass cover and touching the face. It had two raised bars at the twelve, and one bar at the three, six, and nine positions. The rest of the numbers were marked by a single dot. The hands were thick and sturdy.

"It looks good on you."

"Thanks. I love it. I've never had a watch before. I have one clock back home that chimes the time every quarter hour. And, of course, the Shepherd had loads of stuff to help with all kinds of disabilities."

"Let me try."

She held out her arm. I closed my eyes and touched my fingertip to the watch. Nothing. I don't know how she could tell time with that. I couldn't even decipher which bumps were the hands and which were the numbers. "Nope."

I pulled out of the parking lot and asked, "Scarlett, do you know what time it is?"

She chuckled and felt her watch again. "Two-oh-eight."

Impressive. She was right on. "You're a genius."

"Just now figured that out, did you?" She reached her hand over and rested it on mine.

"I was thinking, maybe we should stop by Dr. Wyden's clinic and just see what they can do."

A little frown crossed her face, and she pulled her hand away. "They can't do anything for me. I don't have a degenerative problem. Born this way, wasn't I?" She sighed. "I've never seen the color of a rainbow or the sky or a Christmas tree. But I imagine them in my mind, and I don't know if I want that changed." She ran her hands through the back of her hair, smoothing it. "I've been to places like this before. Not with computer chips but other gimmicks. Not really my thing."

"But if you could see, wouldn't you want that?" Who wouldn't choose partial sight over darkness?

"I do see, in my own way." She put her hand on my face. Very distracting when driving. "I can see you are worried, that you didn't shave, and that you're squinting in the sun. Do you want to borrow my sunglasses?"

The clouds had finally given way, and shards of sunlight reflected off the wet road. How did she know all of that?

I parked the car in front of the two-story clinic. Vinyl lettering on the front door read *Center for Vision Repair, Dr. Anne Wyden.* Shouldn't there be some letters after her name? Like OD or MD or both?

"Brought me here anyway, didn't you?" Scarlett asked.

"Let's just go in and ask for a brochure. They won't talk to us because we don't have a parent. You can't do anything in this country without a parent or legal guardian."

"Let me see if I have time." She smiled and checked her watch. "I guess I can spare a few minutes."

I jumped out, trotted around the car, and opened her door for her. We walked into the clinic and up to the reception desk. A young girl with white-blonde hair sat behind the counter chatting on the phone. She held up a finger, indicating we'd have to wait.

The reception room had a few plush couches and lots of reading material in special, large-print editions. Nothing in Braille though. Everything looked new and expensive but still smelled like a doctor's office.

She hung up the phone and smiled at us. "Hi, I'm Jenny. Do you have an appointment?" She looked about five seconds older than me.

"No, we just wanted some information. Do you have a pamphlet or something on the silicon chip procedure?" I asked.

"Dr. Wyden isn't usually in on Saturdays. Would you like to schedule a consultation?" She grinned up at us.

"No. We're wondering about the retinal surgery and if you have something we can read about it." I held up the little pamphlet from the vision store. "Something more than this."

"I have her business card." She handed me a white card with a name printed in large, black ink. "It has her contact numbers and website. Do you want two cards?"

Scarlett snickered.

"Um, no," I said. "We only came in for some information about the eye operation. You know, the basics of what Dr. Wyden can do and who is eligible, that kind of stuff."

"Oh." She twirled the end of a pencil in her hair. "Well, I just work here on the weekends. The regular scheduler is here on Mondays if you want to call then and set something up."

Scarlett stepped up to the counter. "Look, we don't want an appointment. We're here to gen up, savvy? What can you tell us about Dr. Wyden?"

Apparently, she did savvy, at least that last part, because she smiled and said, "Let me think. She lives on the west side. She drives herself to work. Oh! She has a nine-year-old daughter that's blind. That's why she became a visual doctor."

Visual doctor? How did Jenny land this job?

Scarlett snickered again.

The receptionist leaned in and whispered, "But I think she and her husband are separated. I'm pretty sure that's right because they don't have the same last name, and he lives in a totally different country." She smiled at us like she'd just given us an early Christmas present. She looked at Scarlett, and her eyes went wide with enthusiasm. "I love your hair."

"Thanks," Scarlett said, obviously not flattered.

"So did you want to schedule an appointment? Dr. Wyden *is* here today, but she's just doing research and not seeing patients. I have openings on Monday?"

A woman's voice called out from the back of the building, "Jenny, is Gary here?"

Scarlett dove to the floor in front of the counter.

"No," Jenny said. She stared at the air where Scarlett used to be standing then looked at me. "Gary is her brother. Um, is your friend okay?"

"She's fine. She just had to . . . tie her shoe."

Jenny nodded. "Do you want me to tell her you're here?"

Scarlett tugged on my pant leg, and I looked down. She was shaking her head.

"Nope," I said. "But thanks for your help." I squatted down to Scarlett's level. "What's up with you?"

"That's the woman," she whispered.

"What woman?"

"From my dream. The one in the operating room." The words came out in a hushed scream.

I checked the photo on the cover of the pamphlet. I guess it matched Scarlett's description. Scarlett must have recognized her voice. Time to go.

"Who's here?" Dr. Wyden asked, appearing from the depths of the clinic. She did have a deep and soothing voice, just like Scarlett had said.

I flipped Scarlett's hood up and grabbed her hand. I pulled her from the floor and attempted a casual exit. When I opened the front door, a gust of wind rushed in and blew her hood off, exposing Scarlett's telltale pink hair.

"Scarlett?" Dr. Wyden called. It was a question, like she really didn't know.

CHAPTER ELEVEN

CHRISTIAN VS. THE DETECTIVE

I TIGHTENED MY GRIP ON Scarlett, and we bolted for the car. I practically picked her up and tossed her into her seat then darted around the car and jumped in. I slammed the gears into reverse, and when I looked over my shoulder, Dr. Wyden was standing in the doorway to her clinic talking on her cell phone.

I burned about six months of rubber off my tires peeling out of the parking lot. "What was that all about?" I asked.

Scarlett fumbled with the seat belt, trying to keep herself steady as I zoomed away. "It's her. I'm sure of it. I dreamed about her twice, and I'd know that voice anywhere." She panted like she'd just sprinted the whole twenty-six-point-two. "Are they following us?"

I checked the mirrors and didn't see anything that looked suspicious. "I don't think so. I'll drive around a bit and make sure."

After about fifteen minutes of twisting and turning my way through downtown Portland, Scarlett's face took on a greenish tint.

"I still don't see anyone behind us," I told her.

"Good," she said. "Can we drive in a straight line for a while before I puke?"

"Sure. I'll take you home." I made a gentle U-turn to get us going in the right direction. "Did that clinic feel at all familiar to you? Do you think that's where they might have locked you up?"

"I'm not sure, but I don't think so. The building I was in felt much more peaceful, if that makes sense. Not so crowded into the city but a quiet place with trees and a garden."

It had to be nearly ten miles from the clinic to the cemetery. And through some pretty rugged terrain. She would have had to cross at least one highway and maybe two. They must have had another facility. "Do you think we should go back to Detective Parker and tell him we found Dr. Wyden?"

"And say what, exactly? I could tell him about my dream, but honestly, people don't believe in that stuff. 'Hey, Detective, we found the crazy doctor who killed me in my dream.' I don't think so."

True. We'd probably just get arrested again, for defamation of character or some other ridiculous charge. Parker didn't seem overly concerned about Scarlett's kidnapping. I doubt he even believed it.

"No to the police station, then." I took us home by way of Chinese takeout. Scarlett was hungry. Again. When the last of the orange chicken was gone, we settled in on the couch. But I couldn't get Dr. Wyden's eye surgery out of my mind.

There had to be a reason for the kidnappers to target Scarlett. Did they want blind people to experiment on with their new retinal technology, or was there more? The old man at the store said Scarlett wouldn't qualify for the operation, so why bother to bring her here all the way from the UK? What was Dr. Wyden really up to? Or was Scarlett right—the London policeman narked on her, and Connor and Deepthroat didn't want to risk the chance that Scarlett would identify them? I couldn't imagine that the cops in London would be in cahoots with the Portland PD. There had to be a better connection.

"What's the deal with Shepherd Hill School? Did Dr. Wyden ever go there?" I asked.

"Not that I know of. In my dream and at the clinic are the only times I've ever seen her." She grinned. "I don't mean *seen*, but . . . well, you know."

"You said Katie wasn't blind. Why was she at your school?" I couldn't see the reason why Dr. Wyden would want both of these girls.

"Oi! It's not a school for the blind, it's a school for the gifted. Everyone there has something special." She lowered her voice. "Or at least, something different."

"Different how? Like other disabilities?" Maybe they just preyed upon girls they thought were weak. Although, despite her small size, I'd never classify Scarlett as weak. She was probably the strongest girl I knew. Who else could survive all that she'd been through?

"No. Different as in gifted. You know how they say if you lose one sense other senses get stronger?"

"Yeah, I've heard that." I believed it too. Scarlett noticed as much or more without her eyes as I did with mine wide open.

"Well, at the Shepherd, they find people whose disability has elevated their other senses. Only they call it a gift."

"And your gift is that you dream people's deaths before they happen?" Hardly a gift. More like a curse.

"Yes."

"What was Katie's gift?"

"I already told you. She was a genius. *Is.* She can do anything with a computer. She practically put the tech guy out of a job. She was constantly inventing things. She said she was going to invent something to make her rich. Then we could live together and never have to worry about money again."

"What was her disability?"

"She was born with a brain tumor. When she was still young, they tried to remove it, but they damaged her hearing. She was completely deaf in both ears. She had a cochlear implant, but she wasn't satisfied with the way it interpreted sounds. I've no idea what she did or how it operated, but she figured out a way to improve the sound quality to almost normal. And at the same time made the device half the size."

Not that I was any kind of hearing-aid expert, but that seemed like it could be worth some money. "Maybe Dr. Wyden wanted to steal her invention. That would explain why they took Katie. That clinic today wasn't exactly crowded with patients."

Scarlett thought for a second. "I s'pose. Then they could afford to hire a receptionist with some brains in her head."

I laughed. "She was every blonde joke all rolled into one."

"Hey, don't knock blondes. That's my real hair color."

"Serious?" I'd assumed the black in the back of her hair was the natural color. I looked at her hair and couldn't find any light-colored roots like the goth girls at school had. Plus, Scarlett's eyebrows were dark. "You're lying."

"You're catching on nicely. Not as thick as I thought."

"Thanks for that vote of confidence." I shook my head. "How many kids went to your school?"

"Dunno." She tipped her head to the side, tucking her hair behind her ear. "Maybe eighty. Not a lot. It costs a bomb, so only the wealthy families can afford to send their kids there. And even then, only if they've been invited."

But Scarlett didn't come from a wealthy family. "Then how'd you get in? No offense, and if you don't mind my asking."

"They take a few charity cases each year. Katie and I were the charities."

"But you weren't the only blind student, right?"

"No. There were loads." Scarlett yawned and put her head back. She flipped her watch open and felt it. "Nearly eleven. Shouldn't your dad be home by now? On a Saturday?"

If she was trying to shift the focus from her to me, I wasn't going to let that happen. I'd told her enough at the cemetery. I didn't want to go there again. "Gloria's out of town, and there's nothing here he wants to come home to." Truth was, he probably would be home soon, and I didn't want to see him. I faked a loud yawn. "I'm going to bed." I stood up and asked, "Are you coming?"

She cocked her head to the side and grinned. "I thought you said you have boundaries."

"I don't mean . . . you know. In *my* bed. Just, do you want help up the stairs to your bed? Room." I needed to turn down the thermostat; it was hot in here.

"Sure." She chuckled and held out her hand. I hooked it onto my arm, enjoying the way it felt there.

* * *

I woke tired and groggy a little before nine. It had taken me a long time to fall asleep. Scenes of Dr. Wyden and her death clinic dueled with scenes of being locked away for murder—life without parole. I'd tossed and turned until the small hours of the morning before finally finding deep sleep. At least Scarlett seemed to make it through the night without incident.

Dad's voice wafted up the stairs, trespassing into my room. Even on a Sunday he would have normally been gone by now. I crept to the top of the stairs and listened. He was talking with Scarlett in the kitchen. I couldn't make out what they were saying, just unintelligible chatter and an occasional laugh from Scarlett. I sat on the top step.

I liked Scarlett a lot too, but why was she palatable to him and I wasn't? What had I done to be so distasteful that he could talk with her, have a normal conversation with her, but never with me?

"Bye, Mr. Morris," Scarlett said.

The door into the garage opened and closed. A few seconds later, his engine revved and he backed out of the driveway.

Scarlett emerged from the kitchen into the hallway then climbed the stairs. "Watch it," I said.

She jumped. "What are you doing?"

"Sitting here."

"Spying?"

I really couldn't imagine what they'd have to say to each other. I had no idea what my father spoke of with anyone, except a little bit with Gloria. I rubbed my tired eyes. He'd known Scarlett for five minutes and already preferred her to me. "What were you guys talking about?"

"Nothing. The weather. How I slept. The price of tea in China."

I clenched my jaw. The fact that he had nothing particular to say, that he engaged in idle chitchat, only made it worse.

Scarlett reached out until her hand touched my face.

I pushed it away. "I'm gonna go shower."

I let the hot water ease my tense muscles. I shouldn't be mad at Scarlett for my dad's offenses. It wasn't her fault. But in the short time she'd been here, he'd given her more than he'd given me in eight years. Why did he hate me? Why could he love everyone except his own son?

I couldn't let myself think like that. It was this train of thought that had led to me raiding Gloria's meds and ending up facedown on the tile floor. *There's nothing wrong with you*, Jay constantly told me. *There's something wrong with your dad.*

"It's not me, it's him. It's not me, it's him." I repeated my mantra under my breath until I no longer felt like strangling someone. I turned off the water.

When I stepped out of the shower, Scarlett stood in my bathroom, arms folded, leaning back against the counter.

"Dude, come on!" I snapped. "I'm naked." I groped for my towel and wrapped it around my waist. "I thought you finally understood the whole boundaries thing."

"Don't worry." She grinned. "I didn't see anything." She didn't even have the decency to wear her dark glasses.

Note to self: Lock the bathroom door.

"Detective Parker is here to see you," she said without leaving.

I jerked my head up. Did he come to arrest me? Maybe the other guy, Deepthroat, had gone in and lied about what had happened with the waitress too. "What does he want?"

"Dunno. He asked for you."

Then it hit me what Scarlett had done. "What were you thinking? Opening the door to a stranger. It could've been them!" She might have been stolen right from the house. I didn't doubt they knew where I lived. I'd been relying on Dad's security measures to keep us safe long enough to get her home to England.

"I'm not a git. I checked before I opened the door."

"How did you check? Never mind." Not the moment for a lesson on life skills of the visually impaired. I shook a finger at her. "You do not open the door. Not alone. Ever. Okay?"

"Fine."

"Just, let me get some clothes on, and I'll be down." I reached for my deodorant, but Scarlett didn't exit. How could I get ready with her staring at me? "Okay, you have to leave. I know you can't see me. But I can see you, and it's freaking me out."

"Right you are, gov'nah." She turned and left the bathroom and then busted up laughing. How could she be so jovial when I might be on my way to death row?

I threw on a long-sleeve T-shirt and jeans and met Scarlett and the detective in the kitchen. Scarlett had the detective seated at the counter.

When I entered, she was saying, "Sorry I don't know how to make coffee or anything, but— Oh, here he is."

Detective Parker rose and shook my hand. "Christian, nice to see you again."

Yeah right. At least he didn't have his handcuffs at the ready.

"Is your dad here?"

"No, he already left for work." Thank goodness. No way was I up for double team.

"He goes to work on Sunday?"

"He's a very busy man."

Parker nodded thoughtfully. "I just came by to tell you that you've been cleared in the death of Addie Bolton."

"The waitress?" Maybe it wasn't going to be such a bad day after all. "Why? Did you catch Connor and his friend?"

"No. Actually, we went through the charge receipts from the restaurant based on the time of your visit. We tracked down a few other patrons, and they corroborated your story. With the witness's motives in question, there's not enough evidence against you."

There was never *any* evidence against me. "Will this be on my permanent record?" I really didn't want this stupid mess dragging behind me for the rest of my life.

"No. Especially because you're a juvie. We didn't even take your mug shot, did we, slugger?" He was all smug again.

He'd told me at the jail I was only detained, but I didn't know for sure what that entailed.

"Have you had any trouble since the Lloyd Center?" he asked.

I glanced at Scarlett. "No." I decided not to tell him about Dr. Wyden. *Scarlett met someone from her dream* didn't exactly count as trouble.

He nodded. "Well, tell your dad I'll keep the surveillance up for another twenty-four hours, just in case."

Wait, what? "Surveillance? Are you following me?"

He seemed surprised. "No. I've had some uniforms posted outside since Friday, watching the house. In an unmarked vehicle, of course. Your father insisted."

Scarlett gasped, and I staggered back, sitting down hard on a high-backed bar stool. I stared at Detective Parker with my mouth hanging open. "*My dad?*"

CHAPTER TWELVE
CHRISTIAN VS. REALITY

MY FATHER, RICHARD MORRIS, HAD requested a police guard to protect me? I shook my head. No way. He must've been worried about the house. Or even Scarlett. Parker probably told him everything, including the part about the kidnapping. My dad wouldn't want something like that on his hands. How would it look down at Morris and Clarke if a teenage blind girl went missing from his own home? He cared about keeping up his image.

That also explained why the dynamic duo hadn't come crashing through the front door yet. All this time I'd been thinking we were kept safe by the gate at the bottom of the street and Dad's high-tech security system. How could I be so naïve?

Scarlett rested her hand on my arm. "Thanks for coming, Detective."

I sucked in a quick breath and tried to salvage my composure. "Yeah, thanks." I suddenly liked him better, now that he'd taken me seriously and gotten me out of a murder charge. "Thanks for looking into the whole witness thing. I really didn't want to go to jail again."

He gave me a nod but continued to study me through narrowed eyes. He'd probably just assumed my dad actually communicated with me like a normal father. "No problem, sport," he finally said. He turned his attention to Scarlett. "We've also been looking into your kidnapping claim, since the two are obviously related. We don't have much to go on, other than the description of the men who assaulted Christian in the restaurant and the name 'Connor.' Are you positive you don't have any other details you can share?"

I thought for sure she'd mention Dr. Wyden, but she didn't.

"No," she said.

She still didn't trust the police. She believed her crazy idea that some kind of international *abduct kids from the Shepherd School* ring was going on. After today's visit, I trusted Parker. And I wanted Scarlett to be safe.

"Actually, something weird happened yesterday," I said, fishing out the little advertisement from my pocket. I slid it along the countertop to the detective. "We went to a place called the Center for Vision Repair, just—well, it doesn't matter why. Anyway, the lady there, Dr. Wyden, she seemed to recognize Scarlett. Really gave Scarlett a scare."

Parker read the brochure, flipping it over front to back.

"I just thought it was odd, you know, that she could identify Scarlett. I'm not sure if that means anything." There. I'd told him about Wyden without bringing up Scarlett's death dreams. She should be okay with that.

"Did you speak with her?"

"No, we just spoke to the receptionist. About the eye stuff. The Wyden lady came out as we were leaving. I heard her call Scarlett's name, but then we drove away."

He pocketed the flyer with a nod. "We'll look into it."

I walked him to the door and peered out, checking the neighborhood for an unfamiliar car. One house down and on the other side of the street, two men sat in a dark-blue Crown Victoria. I waved, and they waved back without smiling. Bored to death, no doubt—babysitting a stupid rich kid.

Some protector I was. A strange car had been parked on my street for two days and I didn't even notice. What if it had been Connor? It was a miracle Scarlett was still alive.

"Well," Parker said. "Let me know if you need anything."

"Okay."

Parker climbed into a black Dodge Charger and pulled away. He tossed a head nod to the cops as he passed.

Scarlett waited for me in the kitchen, still sitting on the bar stool, leaning on her elbows over the counter. "That was pretty cool of your dad. To get us a watchdog, I mean."

I shrugged. "I guess."

Scarlett cleared her throat. "He seems nice."

"Parker?"

"No." She grunted. "Your dad."

And that right there was exactly why I didn't tell people about my problems with my father. He could charm the socks off of anyone. "Of course he's nice. To you. To the detective. To people he wants to impress."

"But he said—"

"Look. You've been here, what, thirty-six hours? I've lived with him my whole life." I stood up and started pacing back and forth between the sink and the refrigerator. "Do you think it's easy for me? Watching him smile at everyone else? Watching him take an interest in someone else's life but never mine? Why do you think he insisted on surveillance?"

She shook her head without looking up.

"Because he likes *you*, Scarlett. Not me. Because he doesn't want his name in the papers if you go missing again. Because he wants Detective Parker to know that he has some power in this stupid city and that he knows how to use it. Not because of me."

Her fists curled up into balls, but she kept her face down, like she was studying the stone pattern in the granite countertop.

My voice rose, filling the kitchen with heated words. "He hates me. He can't stand the sight of me. He wishes I had never been born. I lay unconscious for over twelve hours on my bathroom floor, and he never knew." I leaned over the counter beside her. "So don't try and convince me he's this really great guy. You don't know anything."

She lifted her face, and her lips were pressed into a thin line. "Don't tell me what I know and don't know. I'm sorry your life has been such a bugger. Must be rough not having loving parents while you drive around in your fancy car and sleep in your giant bed. At least you have a place to stay without bumming flat space from your friends."

I stared at her. "So now it's a competition for whose life bites the most? You're blind. You won the day you were born."

She dropped her forehead onto her crossed arms and whispered to the granite, "Doesn't feel like I won."

"Well, then, I'll buy you a gold medal so you can feel better." I fled the kitchen and pounded my way up the stairs to my room. I stood in front of my window, looking toward Forest Park in the direction of my mother's grave. People always thought that because I had a handful of cash, all my problems would be solved. I was sick of it. Sick and tired. I flopped backward onto my bed and stared at the ceiling.

I thought Scarlett saw past all that. Beyond the money and the lifestyle to the real me. Maybe buying the clothes and the watch was a mistake after all. I just wanted her to be happy. I shook my head at the irony. I knew better than anyone that having nice stuff and happiness were not connected.

I lay there for a long time with my eyes closed. I heard some dishes clanking in the kitchen. Scarlett was getting herself some food. I should've gone down to help her, but I didn't. Truth was, she didn't need me. Pretty much no one did.

I must have dozed off for a while because when I opened my eyes, the sun had crossed to the other side of the house, leaving my room in cold shadows.

Or maybe it was guilt that made me shiver. I shouldn't have blown up like that. She didn't do anything wrong. *Don't be like him*, I reminded myself.

I went downstairs to check on her. To apologize. With any luck, we could still be friends.

She sat on the couch reading her book, her pink halo of hair just cresting the back of the leather cushion.

Her face turned partway in my direction as I approached. I took a seat beside her.

"Scarlett," I said in a soft voice. "What am I supposed to do with you?"

She sighed and closed the book. "I know. I should go. You've been very kind."

She thought I wanted to get rid of her. "That's not what I meant. Parker said the police will only watch the house for one more day. It might not be safe here after that. I don't want them coming after you again."

She nodded. "You could just take me back to Detective Parker. He can help me get home."

"You hate the police," I said. She was still mad. She had her dark sunglasses barrier back in place—she hadn't worn those for a while.

"I'm thinking the sooner I leave, the better."

"Scarlett." Did she really mean that? I'd only known her a few days, but I felt closer to her than anyone. Not even Jay knew about the overdose thing. It seemed to me that running for our lives from two kidnappers was sort of a bonding experience. But maybe she didn't feel that way. Maybe she saw what everyone else saw, that I wasn't really worth it.

It didn't matter anyway. She'd have to go home eventually, and probably sooner *would* be better—for her own safety.

"Let's wait until tomorrow. If it seems all clear, we'll figure out a plan."

"Yeah. Brilliant," she said quietly.

It didn't seem that brilliant to me either. I'd devised a plan to procrastinate a plan. But what else could I do? Except make amends for the kitchen scene.

"Scarlett, I'm sorry."

She took her sunglasses off and set them on the couch beside her Braille book. I took that as a good sign. But she didn't say anything.

"I'm sorry I yelled. I was tired. I was bugged because of my dad. I shouldn't have taken it out on you. You deserve better."

She still didn't speak. She just sat there staring at the wall with the phantom of a frown across her face. Finally, her expression cleared.

"It's okay." She rested her hand on my leg. "I'm sorry too. I didn't mean what I said."

"So you don't want me to hand you over to Detective Parker?" I teased.

She grinned. "Well, he's not so bad for a Yank. But I'd rather stay with you."

There was my Scarlett. She was back. I pulled her in and kissed the top of her head. "Thanks."

"Berk," she said but made no attempt to move away.

"So what do you want to do now?" I asked.

"What do you usually do on a Sunday afternoon?"

Well, thanks to Parker's visit this morning, we'd missed church. On a normal Sunday at this time, I'd probably be at Jay's house for dinner. I hadn't turned my phone on to check it since the Lloyd Center. My inbox was probably jammed with messages of panic from Jay. He always went into overprotective mode if he thought I was anywhere near falling away from the Church again. *Note to self: Send a calming text to Jay!*

Or about this time, I'd be sitting home alone watching TV. Even on Sunday Dad worked until nine thirty or ten. Occasionally, Gloria watched with me. We were on civil terms. She knew I struggled with her, and she seemed understanding about it. She was careful not to interfere. I was fairly certain she also knew Dad didn't really love her, but he liked Gloria more than me, and that pleased Gloria.

"I guess nothing. Pretty boring life," I said. "Maybe watch a game."

"That's fine. I'll read while you watch."

She picked up her book. The cover was plain white paper with no picture, just a group of raised dots in the center and the title and publishing information in print underneath. The larger-than-notebook–size pages had a black plastic edge thing holding them together, like it had been bound down at the local copy center.

The papers were solid white with Braille bumps in rows. She opened the book flat across her lap and ran the fingers of both hands over the paper. She turned the page and kept going, moving quickly across the bumps. Then she stopped and moved back and forth a few times over the same set of dots.

"What's this word?" she asked.

I shook my head. "I don't know. There's no print at all. I'm sorry I'm so useless."

"Get off," she said with a laugh. "I'm just taking the Mickey. I could feel you watching me."

"How can you even read that?"

"Like this." She took my hand and placed it on the page, then she put her fingers in front of mine. She slid our fingers across the Braille, reading aloud.

How could she form those dots into words? It felt like nothing to me. Like the bumpy surface of a basketball. Maybe there are subliminal Braille messages on basketballs. Had anyone checked on that?

"You're a genius, really. I can't feel anything." Actually, I was feeling something, but it didn't have anything to do with Braille. Her body, small as it was, fit perfectly next to mine.

She transferred her mystic reading powers to me and put her fingers on my face. Every time she did that, my blood boiled. I lifted her hand off. "You know, that's not really fair."

"Blind from birth, yeah? I don't have to be fair."

Ugh. Did I really say that? Why was I such a dimwit? "Scarlett, I didn't mean that. I'm an idiot."

"S'pose I should disagree, shouldn't I? But sometimes you are a bit daft." She placed her soft touch back on my cheeks then ran her fingers through my hair.

I leaned down and kissed her, putting my arm around her shoulders. She closed her book and set it carefully on the floor while at the same kissing me with very effective enthusiasm.

The doorbell rang, and both our heads jerked up, instantly alert.

"Are they here?" she asked.

"I doubt it. Not with the cops out front." Maybe one of the policemen needed the john or something.

I went to the control panel on the kitchen wall and pressed the button to view the front door. A man stood on the front steps, waiting. He didn't wear a uniform, so not one of the surveillance team.

"I don't recognize him," I said.

"What do you mean?"

"We have security cameras. I can see him outside, and it's not someone I've seen before."

He rang the bell again and stepped back, looking at the house.

I pushed the speaker and asked in a voice that I hoped sounded like a parent and not a seventeen-year-old kid, "Who is it?"

"My name is Simon Lawrence. I'm looking for Scarlett Becket." He had a British accent.

Scarlett grabbed my arm. "It *is* Simon. I know his voice. Open the door."

"The guy who never answers his phone?"

"Yes." She tugged on my arm again. "The man who let me stay at his flat after I left the Shepherd."

Yeah, yeah. I knew who he was. I checked the monitor again. He looked a little old for Scarlett. Maybe he really was just a friend.

"Christian, let him in. He's my best friend, my only friend."

Best friend? Only friend? Where did that leave me? Did a little kiss on the couch not qualify me for the list of friends? What more had Simon given to make the cut?

She gave up on me and headed for the door, running her hand along the wall.

"Scarlett, wait." I wasn't going to let her answer the door alone. We'd already covered that in the bathroom. "I'll let him in. Let's just go carefully. What if it's a trick?"

"How can it be a trick? I know him like a brother."

Brother? That sounded a little better. "I'll open the door, and you just hang back until I find out what he wants, got it?"

"Fine."

She stood behind the door while I cracked it open about two inches. "What do you want?"

"Hello, my name is Simon Lawrence. I got a call from the police about Scarlett. I'm her guardian, and I've come to take her home."

CHAPTER THIRTEEN

CHRISTIAN VS. THE NIGHTMARE, REPRISE

I OPENED THE DOOR A little wider, and Scarlett slipped past me. "Simon!" she cried.

Simon touched her hand, letting her know where he was. She jumped into his arms. He was shorter than me by several inches but well built. Younger than my father, although definitely older than I'd expected based on what Scarlett had told me.

He hugged her tightly then lowered her onto the doorstep. He kissed her forehead in a rather platonic way and said, "I've been so worried."

I swung the door wide. "Do you want to come in?"

"Thanks." He stepped into the house.

One of the cops from the surveillance car stood on the sidewalk and called, "Everything okay?"

"Yeah. He's her friend from England." I closed the door and ushered Scarlett and Simon into the family room.

Scarlett sat next to Simon on the couch, where we'd just been kissing. I took a seat in the extra chair.

"How did you find me?" she asked.

Simon leaned back and draped his arms across the cushions, crossing his legs. "I got a phone call from an American police officer asking me about Scarlett. If I knew her. If she'd gone missing."

It had to be Detective Parker. He's the only one who knew the whole story. He'd definitely taken me more seriously than I'd thought if he'd called overseas to follow up on Scarlett's situation. Parker must have told Simon she was with me. So he had come to get her.

Simon went on. "I told him I'd been going crazy trying to find her." He ruffled Scarlett's hair. "Never thought she'd be in America though."

"Didn't you go to the police in London?" I asked.

"Course. They were on the search as well. But she had vanished. I'm not sure they were convinced she didn't just take off on her own."

Right. Because so many blind girls set off to make their way with only the clothes on their backs, no friends, and no money. Did they really think she'd just jump on the subway and head out?

"I can't believe you're here," Scarlett said.

"I'm just glad you're safe. You have no idea how scared I've been." His arm dropped from the back of the couch to her shoulders, giving her a squeeze. Another friendly gesture. Maybe Simon really was nothing more than a nice guy helping out a homeless blind girl. Then he said, "I'm sorry to rush, but we have a plane to catch. We need to leave."

It was a sucker punch to the gut. "So soon?" In only three days, Scarlett had wormed her way into my life so completely that the thought of her leaving left a lump in my throat. We'd just established that she'd stay a little longer. I wasn't ready to let her go.

Scarlett frowned. I hoped that meant she was disappointed too. She'd been so excited to see Simon I'd almost expected her to jump up and run for the door, towing him along behind her.

"What time do we have to leave?" she asked, flipping open the glass cover of her watch.

"Wow, brilliant," Simon said. "Where did you get it?"

"Christian bought it for me. And this." She picked up the Braille book that still lay on the floor, set aside during our moment of distraction.

"Nice," he said. "But look at the time. Scarlett, we'd better go."

"Can I take my stuff?" she asked me.

"Of course. What would I do with it?"

She put her glasses on and left the room, taking her book and a large portion of my happiness with her. Her soft footsteps padded up the stairs.

Simon looked at me, and his eyes got a little moist. "Thanks for taking care of her. The police officer told me you had some trouble. I can never repay you for your kindness to her." He wiped an eye. "She seems happy."

I nodded. I should be chatting with Simon. Small talk. But my brain was scrambled trying to remember what I'd done with my life before she got here. "Well . . . she's pretty cool. It was nice to get to know her." We sat in silence a little longer. "Uh, Scarlett talked about you quite a bit," I said then quickly added, "in a good way."

He smiled and nodded.

"We tried to call you. A lot. Maybe your phone was turned off?"

He pulled out a little cell phone from his breast pocket and flipped it open. "Is that so? I didn't get any messages. But this mobile's been giving me trouble." He laughed at it like it was an adorable, disobedient child. "It doesn't work outside the UK anyway."

"So is there a number I can reach her at? I might want to call and say hi sometime."

"Of course. Ring her anytime." He rattled off a long number, and I entered it into my contacts. He said it was the number to the flat. I guess Scarlett didn't have a phone of her own.

Simon leaned forward and spoke quietly, I assumed so Scarlett wouldn't hear. "I know you're worried about her. But I want you to know, I've taken extra precautions to keep her safe. I installed a new lock on the door, and I've taken next week off work, just to make sure things settle down properly. The London police know what happened; they're on the lookout. It won't happen again."

I hadn't forgotten that she was taken from Simon's apartment in the first place. But with Connor and Deepthroat chasing us around Portland, London definitely felt safer than here. How many times could a couple of kidnappers fly back and forth across the Atlantic toting stolen blind girls?

"That's great," I said.

More silence.

He checked his watch and then scooted to the edge of the couch. "Maybe I should go help?"

"No." I stood up. This would give me a chance to say good-bye in private. "You make yourself at home. I'll go check on her."

I jogged up the stairs and opened a hall closet. I found a carry-on with wheels and headed into Scarlett's room. She sat on her bed with her head in her hands.

"What's the matter?"

"Nothing." She stood and walked to the chest of drawers, feeling around until she found the handle and then pulled it open.

"Here's a suitcase for you." I put it on the bed and unzipped it, flipping the top open. "I think it will hold all your stuff without being bigger than you are." I chuckled, but she didn't respond. Usually, jokes about her small stature got a little rise out of her. Not this time.

"Thanks." She turned around, holding a pair of brand-new mangled jeans.

I placed her free hand on the suitcase. She put the jeans in before turning back for something else.

I stepped in front of her and put my hands on her shoulders. "Hey. Talk to me. What's up? I'd thought you'd be glad to go home. You seemed happy enough to see Simon."

"I am happy to see Simon. And I do miss home."

"But?"

"But I'm also sad to leave."

Sad to leave me or sad to leave my money? I'd seen it even before Gloria. It's not like we were the richest family in Portland. There were bucket loads of people with more wealth than us. But Dad could retire now and still be set—very well set—for the rest of his life. That kind of lifestyle is attractive to some women. I didn't think Scarlett was one of them. But after what she said in the kitchen, I wasn't sure. More than one girl at school had tried to attach herself to me because of money.

"Why?" I asked.

She side-stepped around me and placed her folded *Mind the Gap* T-shirt into the suitcase. She held out her hand, an indication that she wanted an exact location of the person she was with. I took it and moved closer.

"Don't you know?" she whispered.

It *was* for me. She didn't want to leave me. I grinned and pulled her in close. *Stay*, I wanted to say. *Stay with me.* But I couldn't. She needed to go home. I'd tried to help her and keep her safe, but I'd made more fumbles than saves.

Connor and Deepthroat would come back. Of that I was sure. This was our last night of police protection. And then what? How many times could we wiggle out from under their net?

"I know." I stroked her soft, pink hair. "I'll miss you too. But I can't protect you. You need to be with someone who knows what they're doing. How many times have I almost gotten you killed? You need someone who can keep you safe." And Simon seemed capable enough.

She put her arms around me and hugged me tight. Her body shook as she tried to hold back the tears. She failed, breaking down and sobbing.

"Please don't cry. You have no idea how hard it is for me to watch you cry."

"What if I never see you again?"

"Look, I'll make a deal with you. If you stop crying, I promise I'll visit. I'll come to you in England. Over Christmas break. You can take me to all the cool places. Deal?"

She took off her sunglasses and wiped her red eyes. For the second time, I saw something in them. They were dark and wide. Not terrified like before, when she'd dreamed her own death. This time I glimpsed sadness or maybe worry. Something more than a temporary good-bye.

"Scarlett. What aren't you telling me?"

"I had another dream."

I shook my head. I hated her dreams. They were beyond nightmares. But I didn't remember her crying out since she's seen her own demise the night before last. I'd been with her ever since. What could be worse than what she'd already seen?

"Remember the night at the cabin when I woke up to go to the loo?"

"You mean when you woke up screaming?" I'd assumed it was another Katie dream, but she'd never told me.

"Christian, I dreamed about you."

I felt the warmth drain from my face. Sucker punch number two. "What did you dream?" I asked, my voice flat and vacant. Based on her other dreams, I was pretty sure I already knew the bottom line.

"In my dream, you were in a cold place. There were other dead bodies around you, at least two, and they were very cold. The bodies were on tables, like the one Katie lay on."

The operating room. It had to be in the eye clinic, even if that wasn't where Scarlett had been locked up.

"There were shouting voices. I think one might have been the man you call Deepthroat. I heard gunshots, and then you fell to the ground. The floor underneath you pooled with warm blood." She finished her dream in a whisper. "I felt your heartbeat slow and stop."

"I get shot?" I sank down onto her bed. How could that happen? She was leaving, and when she drove away with Simon, I wouldn't be involved anymore. Still, my hands were shaking.

"Please don't be mad."

"I'm not mad." It wasn't her fault, was it? I didn't know how the dream thing worked. Did she dream it, and so it came true? Or was it already destined to come true, and so she dreamed it? Both of those options left me with little opportunity to determine the outcome of my own fate. Maybe the dreams were just a warning, things that *might* happen if we didn't do something to change them.

I stood up, put her hand on my face, and shook my head. "Scarlett, there's no way that's gonna happen. I'm sending you home with Simon. He has plans to keep you safe. This whole thing is over. I don't think your dreams are as true as you think they are. They're just dreams. Everyone has bad dreams, and they almost never come true." I had to add the *almost* because some of hers had come horribly true.

She went back to loading her clothes into the suitcase, tears falling freely as she worked.

"Why didn't you tell me before now?" I asked.

She tucked in the last of her stuff—her heavy combat boots—and flipped the top closed. "I was afraid you'd leave me again. I was afraid to be alone."

Another twist of the knife that stabbed my heart. I'd never forgive myself for leaving her on the highway. No wonder she didn't want to mention a death dream involving me. But now that she was leaving anyway, it didn't matter.

"I admit I was stupid that first day. I was angry at the world. But I hope you know by now that I'd never abandon you like that again. Even if you dreamed about my death a dozen more times."

"Do you mean that?"

"After all we've been through? Of course. Why wouldn't I?"

"Everyone who's ever watched out for me has left me. Except for Simon."

"Well, technically, I'm not leaving you; you're leaving me." I wiped the tears from her face. "And I'm not getting shot either. When you go back to England, this whole thing will be over. So stop worrying."

She nodded her head.

I put my arms around her and kissed her.

There was a knock on her bedroom door, and Simon walked in. "Are you ready? We should be off."

He didn't seem shocked to walk in on us kissing, and I wondered if he'd been listening at the door. But he also looked like he didn't care, and that surprised me.

I zipped her suitcase closed and handed it to Simon. "She's ready." I followed them down the stairs and to the front door.

He shook my hand. "Thanks again. I'll take good care of her."

Scarlett gave me quick hug. "Don't forget to call and that you promised to come. And say good-bye to your father for me."

"Yeah, maybe in ten more years he might talk to me again; then I'll be sure to tell him you said good-bye."

She hooked her hand on Simon's arm, and they started down the walkway. She turned her head and called over her shoulder, "Just remember, football is a game of two halves."

The door closed. I turned and stared into the empty house. The fridge hummed softly, and the alarm system beeped once, reactivating itself.

She was gone. Just like that. What was I supposed to do without her? Live here with my father and Gloria, alone and miserable? Having someone interested in my life, someone who cared about how I felt and who actually liked being with me made me hate my dad more than ever. It was easier when I didn't know what I was missing.

I went back into the family room and slumped onto the couch. I switched on the TV, losing myself for a few hours in banal sitcoms. Tomorrow was Monday—school. I'd missed Friday, so I'd need to write a note and sign my dad's name. Or I could run away again. But then I'd be cut off and penniless.

Why hadn't I left home years ago? Why had I wasted my life waiting for something that would never happen? I should have called social services myself and asked for a foster family when I was ten years old. Or asked to live with my aunt and uncle in Canada—where I'd been headed when I left three days ago.

I hadn't made it too far. I'd only gotten to my mother's grave before Scarlett entered the picture. Now she was gone, leaving a void even bigger than before. I'd thought for a moment she might be the bridge between my father and me—if she could have stayed long enough.

He seemed to like her. He spoke to her. He even spoke to me a few times when she was here. He ate with us—at least for a second. I should have known not to get my hopes up. Permanent depression was easier than working your way up only to be crushed down.

I heard the garage door open. He was home. I couldn't face him. Not right now.

I darted up the stairs and shut the door of my bedroom. I switched off my lights and climbed into bed, shoes and everything.

He moved through the kitchen, probably getting his drink and maybe a bite to eat. One good thing about Gloria was that she kept the kitchen well stocked. She didn't cook—not that family dinners had ever been an option—but she packed the freezer with frozen food and kept scurvy at bay with some fresh fruits and veggies.

From there, he usually went straight to his room or his study. He and Gloria rarely hung out in the main rooms. They watched their shows and did whatever else they did in the master bedroom.

His footsteps shuffled down the hall but not in the direction of his rooms. They came to the stairs and started up. I held my breath, listening. The door to Scarlett's room opened and then a few seconds later closed. Now he stood outside my door, the shadow of his feet just visible through the crack underneath.

What was he doing? He never came up here. And this was two nights in a row. The door opened, and I slammed my eyes shut, trying to regulate my breathing in an I'm-sound-asleep-right-now kind of way.

He shuffled across the carpeted floor toward my bed, paused for a moment, and then left, closing the door quietly behind him.

I sat up. What was with him? He should be downstairs drinking his expensive wine, not snooping around my room or Scarlett's empty one.

What did he want? Was he checking on me? He never checked on me. Did he think I'd left again? Of course. When he didn't see Scarlett, he'd figured we'd run off together. He probably needed to know whether or not to cancel the credit cards and car insurance. Most likely, he was already working out the changes in his will. Although, chances were he'd written me out of his inheritance a long time ago.

I kicked my shoes off and rolled over. Some lawyer he was. My car in the garage should've been all the proof he'd needed to know I was still here.

Whatever. Tomorrow, I'd go back to school, and life would be back to its usual daily crumminess.

CHAPTER FOURTEEN
CHRISTIAN VS. PRECALCULUS

SURE ENOUGH, WHEN I ENTERED the kitchen in the morning, my first dose of nausea sat at the counter drinking a chocolate meal-replacement shake—yellow hair, absurdly long for her age, white-tipped nails, and more cleavage showing than appropriate for seven in the morning. Or ever.

"Hi, Gloria." She must've come in pretty late. I was surprised she was up so early. "How was Vegas?"

It seemed she'd been hoping for that question because she gave me a friendlier smile than usual and said, "So amazing. We had the best time. I won fifty dollars at the slots, and we saw Cher!"

My appetite vanished, and it wasn't because of Cher.

"The food! Oh wow! I ate so much I'm on a diet for a year. But we got this great—"

"You know what? I'm totally late for school. Sorry. Gotta go." I slung my backpack over my shoulder and walked straight to my car.

The Rover was still loaded with all my stuff. I guess I should've brought it in since my dad had me financially trapped here. I wouldn't get far without his money. *Note to self: Get a job.*

I drove the fifteen minutes to West Hills High School with my forged excused-absence note in hand. I'd been signing all my own school forms since sixth grade—report cards, field trip permission slips, driver's ed insurance forms. I could have bought my own house if I didn't have to sign in person.

Jay Jackson, star wide receiver of the football team, waited by my locker. He leaned against the chipped yellow paint, one hand holding his notebook and the other tucked casually into his jeans pocket. His curly black hair was still wet from his post-football-practice shower, and his skin was the same chocolate brown as Scarlett's eyes.

"Where were you on Sunday?" he asked.

I knew this would be his first question. He thought I skipped church on purpose. "Have a little faith, dude. I'm not that lame. Something came up, and I couldn't make it."

He glared at me for a minute—trying to read my mind—while I smiled a perfectly innocent smile at him. "Why didn't you answer my texts?"

"I've had my phone turned off all weekend." Which reminded me. I pulled it out of my pocket and turned it on.

More glares.

"What about Friday?"

"I, uh, went to the cabin for the weekend." That seemed like the easiest answer. If I told him I ran away, he'd never let me out of his sight. "Relax, okay. I had an emergency come up. I'll tell you about it later." We had three minutes until first period. I wasn't up for a full-on explanation of Scarlett or the bathroom floor in thirty seconds or less, and most assuredly not in the main hall at school.

"Are you coming to Mutual on Thursday?" He sounded like Detective Parker, grilling me, just waiting for me to slip up.

"Absolutely." I tried to prove it with my most earnest look. "Seriously. I'm totally fine, and we're still good."

He relaxed, his intensity melting away, leaving the old, overexuberant Jay in his place. "You missed an intense game." He flashed a brilliant grin to a gaggle of girls passing by. "Three touchdowns!" He pumped his fist. His personality was almost as big as his talent. He had already committed to the University of Oregon. For him, it was the Ducks or nothing.

"Cool," I said.

"So, who'd you go to the cabin with?" I expected this question. Besides Jay, I didn't have a big pool of friends—not ones I'd take to Hood River. Plus, I never missed his games.

"No one," I said. But I didn't want to lie. "I mean, I met this girl. It's a long story. I promise I'll tell you later."

"You took a girl to your cabin for the weekend?" he bellowed, loud enough for the entire hallway to hear. He shook his head with disappointment.

"Shut up." I said it through clenched teeth. "It's not what you think. I'll tell you. Later."

Beth looked up from across the way. She gave me a disgusted look, slammed her locker door, and marched away. There went my chances with her. That is, if I'd actually had a chance in the first place. Somehow, I didn't mind.

"Fine," he said. "But this better be good."

The warning bell rang. "You coming?" I asked, waving a hand in the direction of the classroom. We both had math first period.

"Yeah." Jay narrowed his eyes and tipped his head to the side. "What happened to your face?"

He had a good eye for injuries. My bruise from Connor had faded, and my lip was almost healed. "I got in a fight."

"Nice. How'd you do?" Jay had a hard time repressing the football player inside.

At the restaurant—not so good. At the bookstore—great. "I broke his nose."

"Not bad for a tennis player." He held up his fist for a bump but then pulled back. "Wait, it wasn't a pipsqueak freshman, was it? 'Cause that doesn't count."

I grinned. "It was a thirty-year-old guy with a gun."

His jaw dropped, and he looked like a jackrabbit caught in the high beams. "No way."

"Way." I shut my locker and walked off. He jogged to catch up as we entered the classroom. Jay kept *psst*-ing at me. I studiously opened my notebook and ignored him until he heaved an exaggerated sigh and gave up.

We sat on the back row in Mr. Consejo's class—precalculus. A monumentally boring subject, but if you got Mr. Consejo off topic, he'd prattle on and waste half the period. And any subject was better than math.

My gaze wandered from the x's and y's on the dry-erase board to the gathering clouds out the window. Scarlett would be home by now. With Simon. He seemed like a nice guy, but I didn't like the idea of her living with him. Did men his age really let young teenage girls stay in their apartments just to be nice? Scarlett insisted they were just friends, and Simon didn't do or say anything to suggest differently.

I could send her some money so she could find a place of her own. Maybe live with a different friend from the Shepherd. A *female* friend.

That would have been a good plan if it didn't mean involving my dad. I'd have to get his help working out the depositing of a monthly payment to her overseas. He'd know how to set it up so Simon and other possible scumbags couldn't get their hands on it.

Not that Simon was a scumbag. I just hated him for taking Scarlett away, even though I knew she was safer there. It was selfish, but I wanted her here, with me. Sunning her face through the car window. The warmth of her little body pressed closed to mine on the couch. Her hands soft on my face.

I yanked my mind back to the classroom. Mr. Consejo wiped the board clean and started a new problem. The markers squeaked as he wrote. "It costs forty-five cents per ounce to mail a letter to Chile." Roberto Consejo was from Santiago, and he tried to work his home country into as many equations as possible. "But it costs sixty-five cents per ounce to mail a letter to Argentina." He didn't like Argentina. Apparently, they were rivals. "If Rosa paid eighteen dollars and fifty-five cents to send thirty-five one-ounce letters to South America, how many did she send to Chile?"

Jay raised his hand. He didn't know the answer. He stank at math. He was going for an interception. "Did Colo-Colo play this weekend?"

Touchdown. The best way to distract Mr. Consejo was to get him talking about his favorite soccer team, Colo-Colo. According to Consejo, they were the number-one team in Chile.

Consejo got a dreamy look in his eyes. "It was beautiful. At least the second half. The first half, not so pretty. At halftime, we were behind nil one . . ."

Halftime. Duh. *Football is a game of two halves.* That's what Scarlett meant. In England, soccer was football.

Mr. Consejo related the events of the miraculous turnaround with mounting excitement. "And with fifty-five seconds remaining— GOOOOOAL!" He shouted it like he was the actual commentator, and a girl on the front row jumped. "We beat Huachipato two to one." He was glowing when he finished his narration.

Two halves. Meaning things can change, there's a chance to turn things around in the second half. Things can get better.

Or worse. I was already at nil. I didn't see any way for the score to change. At least, not as long as I lived in my father's house.

The door to the classroom opened, and a girl walked in, handing a pink note to Mr. Consejo. He glanced at it then looked at me. "Morris, it appears your father is here to check you out."

Jay stared at me. He was the only other person in the classroom who understood the impossibility of that statement.

I shook my head. Nothing on earth could convince me that my dad waited for me in the main office. "No he's not." I didn't mean to say it out loud. A few peopled chuckled.

Mr. Consejo read the note again. "It says here, he is."

I was still shaking my head, my jaw set. It wasn't him. I knew it. He would never come check me out. It would never happen. If they played the

Stanley Cup in the middle of frozen heck, my father would still not come check me out. If a meteor plummeted toward the earth, and all my father had to do to save all humanity from annihilation was come to the main office and get me, he wouldn't do it. "It's not my dad."

Most kids would be running for the door and a chance to get out of class. I sat in my seat, gripping the sides of my desk with white knuckles.

Mr. Consejo walked down the aisle between the rows of students and set the note in front of me. "Why don't you just go down to the office and see." He stifled a laugh.

I closed my books. Who waited for me down the hall? Connor? Or his cohort? Of course he'd know my school. And it'd be a lot easier to get me here than try to get around the surveillance cops—at least until they left at the end of the day.

Scarlett was gone. Didn't they know that? They must. They'd known everything else. Always one step ahead.

"Morris?" Mr. Consejo asked.

"It's not him," I said again. I got up, walked past my snickering classmates, and opened the classroom door, peering down the hall toward the main office. A man with sandy blond hair paced along the wall near the entrance. He had a white bandage across his nose. He saw me and came running at me. The sound of footsteps from the opposite direction told me Deepthroat had been waiting for me in the rear of the main hall, blocking the back way out.

I closed the classroom door and locked it. "Told you so," I said to anyone who cared enough to listen. I dropped my books and ran for the bank of windows.

"Hey," Jay called. "Where you going?"

"It's the broken nose guy," I said and slid out the window while every student in the room gawked at me. They'd be talking about this at lunch for weeks.

I sprinted across the lawn to the student parking lot. When I glanced over my shoulder, I saw Connor and Deepthroat burst out of the school's main doors. Connor's jacket flapped as he chased me. I glimpsed the gun tucked into his shoulder holster. The drawback of living in the suburbs: high schools don't come with metal detectors.

I hit the blacktop and dove behind the nearest car. He wouldn't shoot me here, would he? In front of a school full of witnesses? Stooping low, I snaked my way through the parked cars to the Rover. I jumped in and backed out, keeping my head low.

In Scarlett's dream, I got shot inside the operating room. I relied on her vision to keep calm. *I'm not going to die now*, I told myself, avoiding the implications of what that meant about my future.

I merged into traffic and checked my rearview mirror in time to see them pile into their black Tahoe and squeal out of the parking lot.

The traffic light in front of me changed to red. I pulled into the right lane, ignoring all of the honking, and made a quick turn. This road would take me into quiet neighborhoods. I didn't see them behind me, but a low-traffic area didn't seem like the best way to blend in if they were following me.

I made a series of left turns until I headed in the direction of downtown. My sweaty palms slipped on the steering wheel. When I reached another red light, I wiped them on my jeans.

Why did they still want me? Scarlett was gone—thank goodness. I'd done the right thing in sending her back with Simon. My phone rang, and I knew who it was without looking.

I pushed talk and yelled, "What do you want from me?"

Deepthroat's mellow voice answered. "There's a church up ahead on the right. Turn into the parking lot and we can talk."

I whipped my head around, searching for their car. It was there, about four cars behind me. After this was all over, I vowed I'd sign up for police academy. These guys always got the jump on me, and I was sick of it. I needed proper training.

I'm sure Scarface could've taught me a few things if I'd decided to meet him in the church parking lot. However, more lessons in pain weren't exactly what I had in mind.

"Sure, I'll be right there," I said. The church whizzed by. How stupid did they think I was?

I risked the Rover's paint job and turned left through a stream of traffic. More honking—and I'm sure some unfriendly gestures—followed me. Judging by the second round of honking, so did the black Tahoe.

I wove my way through the busy streets of morning traffic. My phone rang again. "Leave me alone!" I yelled at top volume.

"Sor-ry," Jay said.

"Oh, it's you." Of course he'd be curious. But now was definitely not the time. "I can't talk right now. I'll call ya later."

The moment my call ended, another came in. *I shouldn't answer. I should just drive my car and get away.* But a part of me hoped they'd tell me something, anything that might clue me in as to why they were still after me.

I pushed talk and said, "Oops. I guess I missed the turnoff."

"If you want the girl to live, you'll come with us."

"What?" Did they take her before Simon got her to the airport? No way. They were bluffing, just like when they told Detective Parker I killed the waitress. What time was it in London? Eight hours ahead, so about five o'clock in the afternoon. I hung up on them and called the number Simon had given me for Scarlett.

A car came screeching at me through an intersection, and I swerved hard to avoid it. I'd run a stop sign trying to dial my phone.

In the rearview mirror, I could see them behind me.

"Hello?" Simon said. If Simon was safe and sound in England, Scarlett had to be there too.

"Simon, it's Christian. Can I talk to Scarlett?" Another red light ahead. I turned right without stopping and merged onto the highway, joining the influx of cars headed to the city.

"Christian, I'm sorry. She just left."

I exhaled. So she had made it to London. And with Team Death still following me, it meant they weren't on the next flight to Heathrow. "Where'd she go?"

There was a short pause. "Some friends from school came and took her out. To celebrate her safe return. They went to T.G.I. Friday's. It's her favorite."

They had that there? "Okay, can you tell her I called?"

"Sure." He hung up.

My phone rang again. I ignored it. No more calls until I lost the guys behind me. I wove in and out of traffic, hoping against hope that I'd get pulled over. I owed Detective Parker big-time for the neighborhood watch. Connor would have been in our house in a heartbeat if not for the cops on guard duty.

As soon as I got free from the Tunnel, I exited the highway, twisting and turning my way through downtown. I knew my way around the city pretty well, and the maze of alleys and one-way streets seemed like the best place to lose them. My tires screeched while old women and moms with strollers dove out of my way. I thought I was going to roll a few times.

The black Tahoe followed me. Connor made it look so easy. Gliding through the streets like he was on a leisurely drive. If it weren't for the charcoal gray Range Rover careening ahead, people wouldn't have suspected a thing.

I listened in vain for police sirens to come to my rescue. Where were the cops when you really needed them? I turned down an alley, cut through an underground parking garage, then exited onto the same street I'd just been on. I checked behind me. I didn't see them. I serpentined my way through the streets, careful not to double back and run into them. There was still no sign.

I cranked the steering wheel and pulled into another underground garage. I parked in an empty stall and killed the engine. Ducking my head low, I dialed 911, keeping my finger poised over send in case they found me.

I waited, counting the passing moments by my heart rate. I think it was around a hundred beats per second. My phone rang, and I nearly wet my pants. It was Deepthroat, of course. I switched the power off. The fact that they called me again reassured me more than anything else that I'd finally lost them.

I sat up and glanced around. My mouth fell open. Without meaning to, I'd driven into the parking lot of my dad's building. What kind of sick Freudian slip was that? I'm sure a psychiatrist would have had a great time trying to analyze it. A voice with a German accent—like Arnold Schwarzenegger—spoke in my head: *You are in trouble. Your subconscious mind wants you to turn to your father for help.*

Yeah right. I choked out a laugh. More like my subconscious mind wanted my father dead, so it tried to lead the killers here.

Then Scarlett's words came back to me. *Football is a game of two halves.* Was this halftime?

Dad bailed me out of jail. He called me into his study for a . . . talk. I guess that's what you'd call it. And although the talk didn't go so well—since it ended with a threat—he did ask for police protection.

I could have driven to the police station. I could have gone to Detective Parker. He would have listened to me. But I didn't. I came here. Why?

Arnold was right. I wanted my father to help me.

He couldn't hate me any more than he already does. "What the heck," I said. Might as well give it a try. I stepped out of my car. "Let the second half begin."

CHAPTER FIFTEEN

CHRISTIAN VS. THE VOLCANO

THE PRESTIGIOUS LAW OFFICES OF Morris and Clarke occupied the entire nineteenth floor of one of the tallest buildings in downtown Portland. On the ground level, a coffee shop and other retail stores bordered the sidewalk, accessible from the main lobby or from the street. I stepped into the elevator and pushed the button for my dad's floor.

A woman in a gray skirt and suit jacket called, "Hold the elevator, please." I put my hand out and stopped the doors. She trotted awkwardly, trying to hurry in her impossibly high-heeled boots.

"Thanks," she said, panting after her two-yard sprint.

"What floor?" I asked, letting the doors close.

"Nineteen." She glanced at the control panel and noticed the glowing green button I'd already pressed. "Oh, same as you." She smiled and gripped the handrail.

The moment the elevator moved, I knew I'd made a mistake in coming here. My dad would never change, not after all these years. He always put up a good front, carefully controlling his public image. No wonder he bailed me out of jail; what kind of parent wouldn't? Detective Parker expected a concerned father, so my dad did what he had to do. He played the part. But when the doors closed on the outside world, he was still the same man who wanted nothing to do with me.

I considered pushing another button and bailing out on the next floor, but I'd already said nineteen, and I didn't want to look stupid in front of the spiky-heeled lady.

She kept looking at me. I turned to her and smiled, hoping she'd look away like most people do when you catch them staring.

"Do I know you?" she asked.

I didn't know her, that was for sure. I hadn't been to my dad's offices for eight years. Mom used to bring me here sometimes, when Dad had to work late. We'd grab some takeout food and eat dinner with him in his office. I loved it. "No."

"You're Richard Morris's son. Um . . . Christian?"

I nodded. *How did she figure that out?* I knew I'd never seen her before.

"I'm Madison. I'm clerking for the firm this year."

That still didn't explain how she knew me. "Hi," I said. Now I really wanted to jump ship, but the elevator steadily climbed—bringing my heart rate up with it. The vintage hard-rock song converted to new-age instrumental playing in the elevator did nothing to calm my nerves.

"Are you here to see your dad?"

"Uh, yeah."

"Mr. Morris says you're a model student." She looked on me benevolently.

I worked on producing some sort of smile.

The bell dinged, and the doors opened. "Keep up the good work." She stepped out and disappeared into the mahogany depths of the offices.

How did she know anything about me and my grades? Did she hack into the school's computer? Maybe they kept tabs on the kids of all the important employees. No one wants a bad apple to spoil the reputation of the whole firm. It was the *Mr. Morris says* part that had me confused. The doors started closing again, and I jumped off the elevator.

The reception area was amazing. They'd made improvements since my last visit. Comfortable chairs clustered around coffee tables took up the center space, and a large saltwater fish tank lined one wall. From the huge windows, you could see the northwestern side of Portland, including Forest Park—the big bank of woodland that fingered its way down and separated downtown from the suburbs. That's where our house was. And my mother's grave.

"Can I help you?" a middle-aged lady behind the counter asked. Above her head, standing out against the dark wood paneling in big 3-D block letters, were the words *Morris and Clarke, Attorneys at Law.*

Unless he'd changed rooms, I knew how to find his office. But my courage was rapidly failing. Why had this seemed like a good idea? I cursed Freud *and* Schwarzenegger. I put my hands in my pockets and approached the counter.

"Christian Morris?" she asked, removing the silver half-glasses that perched on the end of her nose.

How did everyone know me? Was there no such thing as privacy anymore? Connor and Deepthroat knew my every move. Jay figured out I wasn't giving him the real story about my weekend. And now this? Strangers I'd never seen before recognizing me out of the blue.

"Are you here to see your father?"

I nodded. Somehow, she knew that too.

"I believe he's with a client, but I'll tell him you're here." She picked up the phone and pushed some buttons.

With a client. I was saved. I wouldn't have to see him after all. I wiped my brow. It would be a little awkward at home, with him knowing I'd come here, but what was one more drop in the sea of awkwardness we swam in every day? I retreated back toward the elevators.

"He says you can go in," she called to me. "Congratulations on making the tennis team."

I spun on my heels and stared, unsure what freaked me out more—that he would see me over a client or that she knew about the tennis team. Dad didn't even know that. "Thanks." My feet were super-glued to the floor. I wished I'd thought this through better before I'd gotten out of my car.

"It's just down the hall and to your left."

"Right. Thanks." I strode off in the direction she'd pointed. When she was out of sight, I slowed to a slug's pace. A man in a dark suit carrying a briefcase nodded at me as he passed. He came from the direction of my dad's office—his dismissed client. My hands shook, and something was wrong with my circulatory system. No matter how my heart pounded, not enough blood reached my brain. My vision blurred, and I shook my head to clear it.

Visiting a father at work should not be this hard. I leaned against the wall to steady myself. Why did I fear him so much? I hated that I stood outside his office having a nervous breakdown. It wasn't fair. Dads should not be the cause of acute anxiety attacks. Or suicide attempts.

It's not me, it's him. It's not me, it's him.

I reached up and rubbed my temples, drilling my hands into the soft tissue until a spark of white flashed across my eyes. I couldn't live like this anymore—all the brutal silence between us. Pretending I didn't care. Waiting endlessly for him to finally look up and see me. Why was I torturing myself? I was a fool to think he would ever be my father. I was betting everything I had on a lottery I could never win.

It wasn't halftime—it was game over. Time for me to grow up and move on. If I didn't get away from him, I knew I'd be back on the bathroom floor. He had let go of me a long time ago, and now I had to let go of him.

I straightened myself, gathering my resolve. Even if he cut me off from his funds, this was the end. I'd go in there and say good-bye and leave him and Dr. Wyden and Connor and everyone else who had messed up my life behind.

I covered the last few feet in one stride and threw open his office door. He stood behind his desk. It looked like he'd been pacing. He seemed surprised that I'd come bursting in. I guess he thought I would knock.

"I'm leaving," I said. Connor and the car chase seemed years ago. I focused on the window behind him, keeping my eyes on Mount Hood in the distance. If I looked at him, I'd lose it. Ironic really, that the best snow in Oregon could be found covering a sleeping pool of molten lava.

He walked behind me and closed the door. "Sit down," he said.

I did, cursing myself for obeying like a masochistic puppy.

"Where's Scarlett?"

Didn't he hear me? Or didn't he care? "She's gone. Someone came from London and took her home." I'd been thinking about her all day, but I didn't realize how much I missed her until he asked about her. I pressed my lips together. I was not going to fall apart like I did on Friday after the jail thing. *Focus on Mount Hood.* Why didn't the heat from the magma melt the snow?

"Are you all right?"

Wow. I'd waited a long time for that question. Now it sounded absurd. Of course I wasn't all right. I couldn't remember the last time I'd been all right. Or maybe I could. Maybe it was sitting on the couch with Scarlett, watching her read her book in Braille. Is that what he was asking about? Was I okay with Scarlett gone?

Focus. Mount Saint Helens. That was another volcano. Not quite as sleepy though. It exploded thirty years ago, spreading ash across eleven states. "Yeah. I just had some trouble at school." Why did I tell him that? *Stupid Freud. Get out of my head.*

"What happened?" He sat down behind his desk and closed the giant law book he must've been referencing with his client. His eyes reminded me of the permanent glaciers on the high slopes of Mount Hood.

A picture frame rested on the corner of the desk, off to his right. I could only see the back of it. I picked it up, curious about what he could possibly want to look at. Gloria? Mom?

It was me.

My senior picture taken a few weeks ago at the beginning of school. How did he get it? I didn't order any prints. I just sat in front of the camera and smiled—it was required for the yearbook.

It was the last thing I'd ever expected to find in my father's office. I stared at it for a long time. Then I turned the picture, showing it to him, and whispered, "Why?"

His eyes locked on mine for a moment then lowered to his desk. "Because you're my son."

I shook my head, blinking back the sting in my eyes and trying to swallow the burning in my throat. I looked out the window. They say that in Oregon, Mount Hood is the volcano most likely to erupt. I pictured a cloud of ash billowing toward the city. I laid down the photo.

This doesn't mean anything. Everyone knew he had a kid. A picture on the desk would be par for the course. The firm obviously didn't know he'd virtually disowned me, and he probably wanted to keep that under wraps in public.

I stood up. "I'm sorry I bothered you." I took a step toward the door.

He jumped out of his chair and strode around the desk, laying a hand on my arm. "Christian." I looked down at his hand, and he dropped it. "Don't leave."

Did he mean don't leave the office? Or don't leave town? Because in my mind, they were the same thing. When I left here, I'd be heading out for good. Maybe Scarlett would take me in in London.

He cleared his throat, "If you tell me what happened, maybe I can help."

"Help?" How dare he say that. After all the times I would have given up everything for one ounce of his help, now he offered it, without apology or shame. I snapped. "Help?" I yelled.

He took a step back.

The muscles in my arms tensed. I wanted to grab the law book and use it to break his nose, just like I did Connor's. I balled my hands into fists to stop myself. Before I walked out of his life for good, I wanted him to know exactly how much he'd *helped*. "How can you possibly say that? You ruined my life."

My voice cracked on every word, but I didn't care. "It's a pretty miserable existence when the only parent you've got left treats you like the plague. Do you know how many times I've wished I was dead?"

He lowered his head, and his shoulders sagged. Did I finally get through? Was it possible he felt something in his frozen heart after all? Good.

I pointed a finger at him, stabbing him right in his sorry heart. "You know what? It would have been better for me if you'd died with mom. I hate you."

He looked up at me, his face void of color. I opened the door and walked out, heading straight to the elevator. The receptionist said something to me, but I didn't turn around. The doors opened with a ding, and I stepped in, out of sight, and slumped against the wall.

The elevator doors slid shut. I sucked in a huge breath and blew it out slowly, then used the bottom of my T-shirt to wipe my face. Now I knew exactly how Mount Saint Helens felt after blowing, releasing all the pressure that had been building for eons. There was a huge crater left behind but also relief.

Now nothing remained between my dad and me. A steel door slammed closed, shutting out all desire to have him in my life. I'd put everything on the table, and he could do whatever he wanted with it. It wasn't my problem anymore. So much for Scarlett's promised second half. This was real life, not a soccer game. What made me think he might change?

Or maybe I was looking at it the wrong way. Maybe my leaving him for good and starting a new life was my second half, my turnaround. The era of my dad was over. From here, things could only get better.

I paused in the main floor by the coffee shop and turned my phone on long enough to call Scarlett. I really wanted to talk to her, to tell her I was finally free. To tell her how much I missed her. No one answered. It was probably too soon for her to be back from her dinner.

Being chased through Portland and then the confrontation with my father, on top of no breakfast, had left me ravenous. I took *hungry* as a good sign—that I was already on the road to recovery. Scarlett would have never made it this long after skipping a meal. I went into the coffee shop and ordered a soda and a sandwich.

I sat on a bar stool at the counter that ran along the side wall and unwrapped my food. I'd stick with the same plan: drive to Canada and see if my aunt would take me in. Without my dad's money, I'd have to get a job and save. If I did well in school, I'd be eligible for a college scholarship. Lots of kids my age had to make it on their own. If Scarlett could do it, so could I.

I'd have to risk going home to get a few things, even though the extra twenty-four hours of surveillance was up. I wanted my computer. And maybe some more cash from the safe.

I glanced up and noticed two men enter the lobby. Connor and his pal, Deepthroat. No way did they follow me here. I knew I lost them in the downtown maze. They must have assumed this was where I'd come. I picked up an abandoned newspaper and opened it to hide my face. Maybe they'd found my car in the parking garage.

They gave a quick scan of the main area, then Deepthroat stepped into a vacant elevator, leaving Connor pacing back and forth across the lobby. I waited, taking bites of my BLT when he wasn't facing my direction.

Several minutes later, the elevator doors opened and Deepthroat stepped off, shaking his head. I strained to hear them, but the hubbub in the café made it impossible to catch more than a few words. I inched closer to the coffee shop door, keeping my head buried in the *Oregonian.*

"The receptionist told me he left fifteen minutes ago," Deepthroat said.

"Did you see the dad?"

"No." Deepthroat took out his phone and held it to his ear. He turned away to speak, nodding his head to whatever was being said by the person on the other end of the line. He flipped his phone closed and turned to Connor. "She says we should wait for him to go home. If he's not there in a few hours, she wants us back at the lab."

They exited through the doors opposite the coffee shop. I followed them and watched through the glass while they climbed into the Tahoe and drove away. They'd parked in a handicapped space.

She. That must be Dr. Wyden. What was she really up to? And how did it involve Scarlett? I risked turning on my phone and used the map feature to locate Dr. Wyden's clinic. It showed the address and phone number. I tapped the number and then *call.*

"Hello. Center for Vision Repair." It sounded like the same girl who was there on Saturday.

"Yes, I'm calling for Dr. Wyden," I said, trying to sound like a responsible adult.

"Oh. I'm sorry. She's not seeing patients today. But you can schedule for tomorrow." Definitely the same girl. What was her name? Jenny?

"Look, I don't want an appointment. Ever. I just want to talk to her. Please tell her Christian Morris is on the phone. I'm sure that will get her attention."

"Dr. Wyden isn't in the center at all today."

"Will she be in later?" If Wyden was out of the office, maybe I could go down and do some investigating. It sounded like I had a few hours before Connor and Deepthroat would meet up there.

"Nope. Not at all today."

"Thanks," I said and hung up before she could offer me another chance to schedule an exam. I powered off my phone again so they couldn't track me.

I turned and started for the parking garage at the exact moment my dad stepped out of the elevator. I tucked my head and kept walking. I'd said my peace. I didn't want to see him again. I had nothing more to say.

He tried to cut me off. "Christian, wait."

I shook my head and kept moving. The door to the parking garage was almost in reach.

He jogged to catch up. "Please, son. Can we talk?"

I spun around to face him. "Don't call me that. You are not my father." I pulled open the heavy glass door and left him standing alone in the lobby. I wanted to forget him. To move on. But I couldn't if he kept popping up. One more reason why Canada—or London—appealed to me.

I left the garage and headed south, back to Dr. Wyden's clinic. I hadn't heard anything from Detective Parker, so either he hadn't found anything at Wyden's place, or he'd chosen not to share it with me. He tended to keep his findings between my father and him, effectively cutting me out of the loop whether he meant to or not. As I understood it, Parker needed reasonable cause for a warrant to search the place, and I didn't think *she recognized Scarlett* counted as reasonable cause. That meant all he could do was ask questions.

I couldn't pass up this opportunity to check it out for myself. I wanted more information about Dr. Wyden's obsession with Scarlett and why she was still after me. Maybe I knew too much. Maybe she simply wanted revenge for my saving Scarlett from her crazy eye experiments.

Scarlett was halfway around the world. Would Wyden try for her again? Now that Simon knew the whole story about Scarlett being kidnapped, he was on the lookout, prepared for another attempt. He promised me he wouldn't leave Scarlett alone until things had settled. He had cops on standby. Was Scarlett right in accusing the London police of being involved somehow?

I called Scarlett again on my way to Wyden's. Still no answer. It would be just after seven in the evening in London. I guess it wasn't unreasonable that she'd still be out.

The parking lot in front of Dr. Wyden's clinic contained only one car. A Honda Accord in faded white—old, rusting, and square. That had to be Jenny's car. No doctor of vision repair would drive such a dilapidated vehicle.

I looked at myself in the rearview mirror before exiting the Rover. My eyes were a little bloodshot; it had been a stressful morning. Not much I could do about that. I ran my fingers through my hair and threw a smile on my face. It'd have to do. I had a plan that I hoped would work. I popped some mint gum into my mouth, opened the front door of the clinic, and went straight to the counter.

"Hi, Jenny. Remember me?"

CHAPTER SIXTEEN

CHRISTIAN VS. THE TOUR

JENNY EYED ME UP AND down and then grinned. "Oh yeah. I do remember you." She punched a few keys on her computer and squinted at the screen. "Did you make an appointment?"

She was obsessed with appointments. It was like she was working on commission. Five bucks for each exam scheduled. I shook my head. "No, I can see fine. I, um." I rested my forearms on the high counter and leaned in. "I actually came to see you." I gave her a jaunty smile, hoping I didn't look like a total nut job. "I thought you only worked on weekends."

I didn't usually spend time hitting on girls, but I knew a few important essentials. Rule number one: maintain eye contact. I might not have been the best-looking guy in school, but according to the poll in my junior yearbook, I made it into the top ten.

"The other receptionist is sick today," she said.

"Lucky for me." The other receptionist could've been fifty instead of eighteen. But by the fluttering of her eyelids, at least I knew Jenny was on board. "So, are you here alone?" Okay, that sounded creepy. I tried to backpedal. "I mean, if Dr. Wyden's not in today, why is the clinic open?"

She shrugged her shoulders. "In case someone comes in."

Right. Jenny may not have been a regular Einstein, but at least she had a nice, friendly smile. I didn't know if I'd call her hot, but she scored in the six or seven range. When she tossed back a lock of her shiny blonde hair, I felt a sting of guilt for leading her on. I already had an attraction to a girl with pink hair. But I really wanted some information, and this was probably my best chance.

"I was wondering if you wanted to go get some lunch." I'd just eaten the sandwich, but it seemed like a logical next step.

"That would be great," she said, then her face fell. "But I can't today. I can't leave the clinic unattended, or I'll lose my job."

I walked around to the edge of the counter and through the door that separated her from the receiving area. "Well, maybe I could hang out here with you for a little while, and you could give me a tour."

She perked up. "Okay."

Wow. That was easy. I noticed a textbook open on her desk. "Were you studying?"

"Yeah. I go to Pacific School of Optometry."

Jenny studied optometry? I guess it made sense—she worked in an eye clinic. But wow. An optometrist? I hadn't seen that coming. How does a girl who used the phrase *visual doctor* become an optometrist? I worried for her patients. "That's pretty cool." I pictured the front door of her office: Dr. Jenny, VD. I coughed to cover my laugh.

"Thanks."

I perched on the edge of her desk. "Why don't you show me around? Let me see what's in store for your future."

"I don't know if I'm allowed."

I rested a hand on the back of her shoulder. "Come on. I've never seen the inside of a vision repair center before. There's not a soul in sight. What could happen?"

"Well . . . okay." She closed her book and opened a drawer, retrieving a set of keys. She waved a hand across the reception counter, encompassing a phone, the computer, a credit card machine, and other office essentials. "This is where we schedule appointments and answer the phone and stuff." She pointed to a wall of shelves, where manila folders with color-coded tabs were stacked. "These are the patient files."

At this rate, it would be time for dinner before she showed me anything useful. Maybe that was her goal. Take it slow and hope for a dinner date.

She gave me a tour of the copy machine, eye chart—where she giggled as she tested my vision: twenty/twenty—restroom, and break room, with a microwave, coffee machine, and full-size refrigerator. She opened the fridge and showed me the medicines stored there. And her lunch, which I told her she could eat if she was hungry. She refused.

There were two exam rooms on the main floor. They seemed pretty basic—filled with machines for vision screening and a big brown plastic-covered exam chair. She surprised me by knowing the names of all of the contraptions and showing me how they worked. Projectors, refractors, keratometers . . . I didn't have eye problems, so I'd never visited an optometrist.

On the counter of one of the exam rooms stood a large, plastic model of an eye. I asked a question I doubted Jenny could answer. "How does Dr. Wyden's eye repair surgery work? What exactly does she do?"

She opened the model to reveal the inside of the eye. "What happens is, some people, when they get old and stuff, their eyes go bad. See the retina—that's this part here"—she pointed to the curved rear area inside the eyeball—"receives the light coming in through the cornea. The retina processes the light and then sends it along to the brain on the optic nerve." She touched the long plastic stem coming out the back of the eye.

Wow again. Between her explanations of the complicated equipment and her knowledge of the workings of the eye . . . I honestly hadn't thought she'd know all that. Maybe I'd judged her too quickly.

She smiled, clearly aware that I was impressed. "A lot of times, it's problems with the retina that cause people to lose their sight. So Dr. Wyden has developed a retinal implant. It's a tiny microchip that she puts just under the retina, and it gets the light signals and processes them, stimulating the working retinal tissue to do the same."

"And then blind people can see?"

"They can see a little of shapes, and it's only black and white."

I never would've guessed, based on our conversation the other day, that Jenny had any idea what Dr. Wyden did. "How do you know all of this?"

"We have to memorize all of it before we can work here. Even as a receptionist."

That explained a lot. "Is Dr. Wyden doing this for her daughter?" I asked, trying to crack into the information that really interested me.

"The retinal implant can only help if someone's blindness is from retinal degeneration. Other stuff, like things with the optic nerve, she can't fix." She put a hand on my shoulder, leaned up on her toes, and whispered, "But she's working on a new implant to help her daughter. It's a secret. I don't think I'm supposed to know. I heard people talking." Her hand rested on my neck, and her mouth lingered near my ear.

I looked at her. She had bright, blue eyes alive with light. Windows. In them, I glimpsed a spark that said *I'm here, and I'm attracted to you.* Something I'd never seen in Scarlett's eyes, no matter how hard I'd searched.

I took a step back and cleared my throat.

She grinned, knowing she'd affected me. "Here, I'll show you where she puts the chips in." Jenny led me to the stairs, and we climbed to the second floor. She took me into a room designed for surgery.

Instead of an operating table, Wyden had an enormous, super-deluxe exam chair. The metal base had a bulge, which I guessed enclosed a motor that ran the hydraulic functions. Various lights and machines were attached to its side, and under the patient's foot area was a built-in set of stainless-steel drawers.

Could this be the room where Scarlett had dreamed her death? Tiles covered the floor, instead of carpet like the rest of the clinic. That matched Scarlett's description.

Jenny took out her set of keys and unlocked a cupboard. "This is the microchip." She showed me a small plastic box with a clear lid. Inside, a tiny black circle the size of a freckle lay on a piece of white cloth.

It was so small. How could that do anything? "That's it?"

"That's it. This is the sample she keeps here to show patients who are interested in the surgery."

"Doesn't it need a battery or something?" I asked. "Where does it get its power?"

"It's, like, solar powered. From the light that enters the eye."

Amazing. I never knew stuff like that existed. What would it be like to go from blind to seeing with just a tiny microchip? Too bad it couldn't work for Scarlett, but what about the new project for Dr. Wyden's daughter? Maybe she was developing a device to give sight to people born blind. People like her daughter. And Scarlett.

So why kidnap Scarlett? For a chance to see, wouldn't she come willingly? And her friend Katie, why take her too? Scarlett mentioned Katie had developed a gadget to help a deaf person hear—or at least an implant that helped Katie hear. Maybe she'd also worked on something for Scarlett. That could be a reason for kidnapping her.

The problem was, other than Scarlett's dream, I had no tangible proof that Wyden was behind Katie's kidnapping—or that Katie had actually been kidnapped at all. Parker had called London, but he'd never mentioned a word about Katie's disappearance. I needed to get into Dr. Wyden's files to find out what she knew about Katie and Scarlett in the first place.

I wandered out of the surgery room and pointed at a door with Dr. Wyden's name on it. "What's in there?"

"That's Dr. Wyden's office."

I checked the door. Locked. "Can we go in?"

Jenny shook her head. "I don't have a key for that room." She jangled her bundle of office keys.

There had to be something in this place that explained Scarlett's abduction and why Dr. Wyden wanted her. I guessed it was in that office. Dr. Wyden could have gotten a blind person from somewhere much closer than London. Why Scarlett?

I jiggled the door harder, and it rattled a bit like it was loose in the frame. "Jenny, stand back." I lifted my foot and kicked the door, right by the knob. It flew open.

Jenny's face went white. "Why'd you do that? You're gonna get me fired."

I checked the door jam and wedged the splintered piece of wood back in place. "Look." I showed her my repair work. "No one will notice. It was already loose. And if you get fired, I can get you a job at my dad's law firm." That was probably a lie. Especially since I'd just made a personal vow to never see him again. But if Jenny's income was her main concern, maybe that would help her feel better.

She looked confused and took a step back. "What are you doing here?"

She really was smarter than I'd given her credit for. And scared. I put my hands on the sides of her head. "Jenny, I need to find something. Someone's life depends on it."

She gave me a questioning look.

"I'm serious. I didn't mean to scare you. But this is important. Can you help me?"

She tipped her head to the side, considering. I saw the same look come into her eyes as before, when she'd whispered in my ear. She'd help me, but a little incentive wouldn't hurt.

I figured, why not? If it might help Scarlett . . . I leaned down and kissed her. Just a quick one on the lips but good enough to make her suck in a quiet breath. I hated myself for doing it. Like I was some kind of gawky, adolescent James Bond toying with her feelings. Maybe Jay was right in his concern for my spiritual safety.

She half smiled and said, "Fine. But you owe me big time."

"Whatever you want. You name it."

Jenny thought for a second. "Dinner. At Andina's."

She'd picked one of the most popular restaurants in Portland, where they served, of all things, Peruvian cuisine. Helping me ransack her boss's office for an experience in fine dining seemed like a fair trade. "Done."

She relaxed a little. "Okay, what are we looking for?"

"Anything about what Dr. Wyden is working on for her daughter." That had to be the connection.

Wyden kept her office tidy and impersonal. A few diplomas on the wall and a framed article about the retinal implant—looked like she'd won some kind of award for it. No photos on her desk. Unlike my father, who kept one of his son.

Jenny dug through the cupboards and drawers behind the desk. I sat down at the computer and switched it on. I'd already been at the clinic for more than an hour. How much longer did I have before someone showed up?

The computer needed a password. "What's the daughter's name?" I asked. "Maggie."

I typed it in. Wrong. If her computer was like mine, I had two more tries before the machine would lock up. I thought for a second and then tried *Margaret*. It worked.

I searched her files, looking for anything useful. Jenny finished with the drawers and leaned over my shoulder, watching the screen and breathing softly on my neck. I found a document titled *Shepherd Hill*.

I opened it. It was the minutes for a board meeting they'd had recently. A few months ago, before Scarlett and Katie had disappeared. I scrolled to the bottom and found a list of all of the members of the board. Dr. Anne Wyden was listed last.

That explained how she knew about Katie and Scarlett. But not why she wanted them.

I checked the e-mails, assuming anything of recent importance would be there. It all seemed like regular office stuff—solicitations from pharmaceutical vendors and insurance companies. She didn't have a lot on this computer, and I couldn't find anything helpful. She had files laden with medical language I didn't understand. And patient files. I checked for anything under Becket. There was nothing. She must keep her private stuff on a laptop or a jump drive.

I pulled open the desk drawers and rummaged through, looking for any kind of USB device.

I found a photograph. A picture of three people. All smiling with their arms around each other. Dr. Wyden. A girl about eight years old. And a man I'd seen before. Simon Lawrence.

I slammed the drawer shut. "Jenny, what's this?"

"That's a picture of Dr. Wyden's family."

My stomach tightened. "Who is this man?"

"That's her husband. And her daughter, Maggie."

Simon Lawrence was married to Dr. Anne Wyden.

I'd let Scarlett walk away with the person who'd kidnapped her. I'd smiled at him and shook his hand, like friends. I'd packed her suitcase and sent her away to be safe with him. She was probably already dead.

In that half second that I'd stared at the photo, everything clicked into place. No wonder Simon was kind enough to let Scarlett bunk in his flat. An easy victim, ready to grab when the moment was right. Who in London would miss a homeless blind girl?

I stood up, letting out a maniacal roar. In one giant motion, I swept everything from her desk. The computer flew off and gouged a hole in the drywall then shattered on the floor.

Jenny screamed and jumped back. "Are you crazy?"

"This is very important. Have you met this man?"

She nodded.

"When was the last time you saw him?"

"This morning. With Dr. Wyden. She came in to say that with her husband in town, she was taking the day off and to cancel all her appointments. But she only had one."

I should've left her on the highway. She would have been fine. Someone would have helped her. Even if I'd taken her suggestion the other morning to drop her off with Detective Parker, everything would've turned out fine. But I hadn't. I'd taken her in my car, tried to keep her safe, and then delivered her into the hands of death.

The front door to the clinic dinged.

"Someone's here," Jenny whispered, looking with horror at the disaster on the floor of Dr. Wyden's office. She left the room and turned down the hallway, out of sight.

A moment later, she screamed. A piercing gunshot cut off her cry.

Jenny! Oh no! I'd stayed too long. They'd found my car sitting in plain view outside the clinic. I recognized Deepthroat's voice instantly as he cursed and yelled—something about trigger happy and not being paid to kill everyone. No doubt Connor had pulled the trigger.

Jenny moaned softly. From the office door, I could see her body lying at the top of the stairs, partially concealed by the wall. I figured I had one nanosecond to make a move before the men came up the stairs after me.

I dashed down the hall, grabbed her hand, and dragged her away.

"He's up there," Connor shouted.

I was rounding the corner into the surgery room when the gun fired again, the noise exploding in my ears. I slammed the door and locked it, hoping it would hold better than Dr. Wyden's.

My arm burned. I looked down. Blood soaked my shirt sleeve, just below my shoulder. Scarlett dreamed I'd die from a gunshot—in an operating room. In her dream, there were two other bodies with me. I only had Jenny, and she was still breathing. But this wasn't over yet.

CHAPTER SEVENTEEN

CHRISTIAN VS. THE CENTER FOR VISION REPAIR

I HEAVED THE GIANT EXAM chair up against the door to brace it shut. Then I pulled out my phone and dialed 911. A pool of blood spread across the white floor tiles.

In the hall, Connor and his friend slammed their bodies against the door.

I grabbed a stack of green surgical cloths from the counter and pressed them on Jenny's chest. She was breathing hard, moaning with every exhale.

"I got you. You're safe now," I lied. I would help her as long as I could, until they broke through the door and killed me. Maybe someone would get here in time to save her.

"Multnomah County nine-one-one. What is your emergency?" the woman's voice on my phone said.

Pound. Pound. Pound. The exam chair slid an inch or so, and I let go of Jenny long enough to slam it back in place.

"A girl's been shot. I need an ambulance."

Pound. Pound.

"What's your location?"

"The Center for Vision Repair. Corner of Gleason and Hawthorn."

A siren wailed outside, and the pounding stopped. That was fast. The 911 operator said something to me. Asked me a question. I didn't hear. I let my phone drop, concentrating on Jenny. Her breathing slowed. She looked up at me. Her eyes were wide and scared, and the light that had sparked in them only a few minutes before grew dim. *Help me*, she pleaded without uttering a single word.

"It's okay. You're gonna be fine." I brushed her hair away from her face. "The ambulance is on its way."

She nodded weakly and closed her eyes.

Her blood soaked the knees of my jeans. I pressed even harder on the wound. More gunshots, from farther away, maybe downstairs. More sirens.

Her chest stopped moving.

"Jenny?"

She didn't respond.

"Someone help us," I yelled. I put my fingers against her throat. Nothing. *Please help me*, I prayed. With one hand on top of the other, I placed the heels of my palms at the base of her rib cage and thrust down in quick succession. One. Two. Three. Four. Five. All the way up to thirty.

I put my mouth over hers, plugging her nose with my fingers.

Breath.

Breath.

Still nothing. *Please don't let her die.* I went back to her chest. One. Two. Three. Four.

A knock on the door. "Christian? It's Detective Parker. Open up."

Nine. Ten. Eleven. Twelve.

"Christian," he called again. Then he yelled to someone else. "I need help with the door."

More pounding, hard and heavy.

Twenty-one. Twenty-two.

The chair slid back, and the door opened a few inches. Detective Parker's face appeared then disappeared. "He's in here. Get the paramedics."

Twenty-eight. Twenty-nine. Thirty.

Breath.

Breath.

A few more heavy slams, and the chair scooted again. A man squeezed through wearing blue rubber gloves and carrying a duffle bag with a large red cross on it.

I put my hands back on her chest and pumped some more. One. Two. Three.

He skidded to the floor and laid his fingers on the side of Jenny's neck. "How long ago did her heart stop?"

Eight. Nine. Ten. "I don't know." I had lost track of time. "Maybe a minute or two." People were still pushing against the door.

He opened a hard-plastic case and pulled out a machine. He ripped Jenny's shirt open and placed the metal plates on her skin. He met my eyes. "Clear," he said.

I let go and sat back on my heels. Her body twitched with the electric shock. More people came through the door. Another paramedic took my place, scooting me off to the side. He gave her a shot of something in her chest. Right into her heart.

Someone pulled on my arm. "Christian. Let's go." I looked up. It was Detective Parker.

"Clear." Her body jerked again.

Parker tugged me to my feet. "Come on."

"But . . ." I couldn't take my eyes off Jenny. How could I leave her here when this was my fault?

"They'll take care of her. Let's get your arm looked at." He pulled me from the room while the second paramedic started CPR again.

A line of red trailed down the hall, a dark smear connecting the dots of her two pools of blood. My hands were covered with it. I stumbled down the stairs, and Parker tightened his grip.

In the back of the clinic, by the emergency exit, another body lay on the ground. He had thinning, sandy-blond hair, a scar across his eye, and a white bandage on his nose. Connor. More EMT guys bent over him. They didn't seem to be working on saving him. He must already be dead.

"Did you shoot him?" I asked without taking my eyes off the lifeless body.

"Yes," Parker said quietly.

I felt the slightest twinge of envy. "What about Deepthroat, the tall guy that's always with him?"

"We're still looking for him. Do you know his name?"

"No."

Parker tugged me along and sat me on a gurney in the waiting room. A paramedic cut a nice, even slit up my shirtsleeve and started working on my arm, washing the wound with stinging liquid. My arm was on fire, but that was nothing compared to the pain in my chest, like the space around my heart was being filled with liquid nitrogen—burning and freezing at the same time.

I plowed my free hand through my hair and said to the detective, "This is because of me. I shouldn't have come here. This is all my fault."

Parker shook his head. "No. It's not. Listen to me." He waited until I looked him in the eye. "Bad people do bad things. It's not anyone else's fault. I see this all the time. Today, it happened here, to you. Tomorrow, it will be someone else. There's no one to blame except the man who pulled the trigger. Do you understand?"

I nodded. I understood what he meant—Connor made the choice to shoot his gun. But if I hadn't been here, he wouldn't have shot it at Jenny.

Who then? Jay? My dad? As long as Deepthroat and the others ran free, everyone around me was in danger.

"You should put me back in jail," I said. "For the safety of my friends."

"Is she your friend?" He nodded his head in the direction of Jenny, up the stairs.

"No." If a deflated balloon could speak, I imagined that was what I sounded like. Limp, empty, withered, small.

The paramedic shined a beam in my eyes, checking each eye twice.

"You were very brave to save her." Parker patted my shoulder in a fatherly way. At least, it seemed fatherly. I wouldn't know from experience. "I need you to tell me what happened. Can you do that?"

I nodded again. Where should I start? From school? From my dad's building? I didn't want to discuss anything about my dad with Parker. "I came here to find out why Dr. Wyden's men were still after me, even though Scarlett went home." I knew now she wasn't home. Just right back in their hands. Had Connor shot her too? No. She doesn't die by gun. She dies on an operating table.

"Did they come to your house?" he asked.

I flinched as the paramedic wrapped a roll of wide gauze around my arm and then secured it with white tape. Already, red showed through the cotton binding. I clenched the fist of my good hand, trying to squeeze away the pain. Pain that I deserved.

"They came to my school. But I got away. I climbed out the window. They followed me into the city." Fast forward. "I heard them say something about Dr. Wyden. I called the clinic and found out she wouldn't be in today."

The paramedic filled a syringe with liquid. He rolled up the sleeve of my right arm, the arm that hadn't taken a bullet, and scrubbed it with an alcohol wipe. "Morphine. You ready?"

I nodded. He stabbed me with the needle and squeezed the burning fluid into my arm.

"So you came here and snooped around?" Parker asked.

"I guess. Jenny, the receptionist, gave me a tour."

"What happened in Dr. Wyden's office?" His tone suggested that I might have taken advantage of Jenny in there.

"Not that. I swear." I pulled the creased photo out of my back pocket and handed it over. "I found this."

He studied it for a few seconds then shrugged. "And?"

"And yesterday, a man came to get Scarlett. A guy who used to work at her school in London. He came to take her home. She's been staying with him for about three months because her mom skipped out. Turns out, it's him." I pointed to Simon in the photo.

"What does this have to do with Dr. Wyden?"

"He's Wyden's husband." I explained about Wyden's sightless daughter and her plans for an improved retinal implant. I told him about Katie and how I thought they kidnapped her so she would design it and that Scarlett was the next test victim. Every word that left my mouth eased the freezing burn in my chest. Now someone else, someone capable, could take the burden of figuring out Wyden's master plans.

"We've got an APB out on the other suspect, based on the description your father gave us. Do you know that man's connection to the deceased or Dr. Wyden?"

I shook my head.

"We'll search this place. Something will turn up that will lead us to him."

The paramedic that first worked on Jenny came out from the back of the clinic carrying his defibrillator. Detective Parker questioned him about her.

He shook his head. "She didn't make it. I put her down as DOA."

I dropped my head into my hand, covering my face. I didn't save her. I didn't save anyone. I lay down on the gurney. "Take me away. Take me away and lock me up."

Parker waved off the paramedics. "Christian, I'm sorry about the girl. But I need you to focus. So we can find Scarlett."

"Scarlett is dead. She already dreamed it. I thought I changed it. But I didn't. And I'm supposed to be dead too, but she dreamed it wrong, and it was Jenny."

"How do you know Scarlett is dead?"

I sat up. "Because she dreams about people dying before it happens. Like a vision of the future. And then it comes true, just like in her dream. That's how she recognized Dr. Wyden in the first place—from her dream. She dreamed that I would get shot and die. And I did get shot, but Jenny died."

I had laughed with Jenny and talked her into helping me go through Wyden's stuff, and look what it got her. Not a nice dinner at Andina's, that's for sure. Just bleeding out on the exam room floor.

I lay back down on the gurney and closed my eyes, waiting for them to cart me away to prison or an asylum or anyplace where this would all be over. The paramedic that had been hovering in the background covered me with a metallic blanket. "I think he's in shock," he said to Parker.

"I'll tell his dad."

My eyes snapped open. "My dad?"

"Yes." He pointed out the front window to the tiny parking lot, where a man with bent shoulders paced back and forth, hunkered into a dark gray overcoat against the drizzle. A ribbon of yellow police tape separated him from the two cops standing guard. Parker, great detective that he was, must have figured out the state of my relationship with my dad. Why else would he be out in the cold instead of sitting on a comfortable leather sofa in the reception area?

"Why is *he* here?" The words spilled out like acid.

"He's here because he's your father. And because he just saved your life."

I sat up again. "What?"

Parker obviously expected this, and his smug smile spread across his face. "After you left your father's office, the man you call Deepthroat came up and asked the receptionist about you."

"Yeah, I overheard them talk about it."

"Well, she told your father, and he called me, worried that you might be into something over your head."

I glanced at my dad out of the corner of my eye.

"I accessed your call log and found the last number you dialed—the clinic. I hurried over in case they followed you."

"I called nine-one-one. I thought that's why you came. But that would have been too fast." It made sense now. Maybe my dad did save my life. I shook my head, not knowing how to process that information.

"They dispatched an ambulance. It was only a couple of minutes behind me. The hospital is just two blocks away."

"Next time, can you get here a little sooner? I could have used some backup five minutes earlier."

Parker chuckled, even though I wasn't joking. "No problem, cowboy." He handed me my cell phone sealed in a plastic baggie. It was coated with blood—a mixture of mine and Jenny's. "Here's a question," he said. "How did you manage to move that surgical chair? It took three of my strongest men to pull it out of the way."

I shrugged and then winced. My arm didn't appreciate the shrugging. "I don't know. I didn't think about it; I just did it. Adrenaline, I guess."

I shivered and wrapped the tinfoil blanket around my shoulders. My arm ached, and the throbbing pain crept up through my shoulder and neck until my head wanted to explode. My hands, still covered in blood, shook.

I must've done something to my ribs trying to shove the mammoth chair against the door; it hurt to breathe.

"Can I go now?" I rolled off the gurney but stood up too fast and my body swayed. Or maybe it was the morphine kicking in. I sat back down.

Parker called the paramedic over. "He wants to go home."

I didn't exactly say *home*. But I did want to leave.

Without any warning, the paramedic opened the clinic door and waved my dad over.

The detective shot me another smug grin and pulled out his phone. He walked into the depths of the clinic, talking on it, even though I didn't think he dialed a number.

When my dad walked through the doors, I lowered my eyes, focusing on the dark stains that covered the knees of my jeans. The last thing I'd said to him was that he wasn't my father. That I wished him dead. Now, according to Parker, I owed him my life. Since I'd entered the Center for Vision Repair just over an hour ago, it seemed my whole existence had turned upside down.

"The bullet went straight through," the paramedic explained to my dad. "In and out without hitting the bone. I patched it up, but you'll have to take him in tomorrow to have it checked. They'll want to start antibiotics to prevent infection. He'll also need a tetanus shot if he's not current. Okay?"

I didn't look up, but my dad must have nodded because the paramedic continued. "Here's some extra bandages. When the blood soaks through, change them. Don't let him shower; it has to stay dry. He can take a bath. Keep him warm, and give him plenty of liquids."

He was wasting his time telling my dad all of this. I stood up again, slowly and holding on to the gurney's metal guardrail. I pulled my keys out of my pocket. "I'll be fine."

The paramedic snatched the keys from my hands and tossed them to my dad. "He doesn't drive for at least six hours. I gave him a dose of morphine."

I groaned. Thwarted again. Every time I saw light at the end of the tunnel, something came along and blocked my view. My plans to escape would have to wait. I braved a quick peek at my dad. He looked pale and tired.

"Thanks," he said to the paramedic. He gripped my right arm and led me from the clinic.

I cast a backward glance at Detective Parker. He was watching us leave, grinning. I saw him mouth, "See ya, slugger."

When we got outside, I shrugged my dad's hand off. I lowered myself into his Mercedes and buckled the seat belt one-handed.

He climbed in and started the car, backing out slowly to avoid the ambulances and police cars. I shivered, and he turned the heat up.

"I'm sorry you had to leave your office," I said, leaning my head back and closing my eyes. The morphine had taken effect, draining away the pain but leaving me tired and spent.

"I don't mind," he said. Then he added in a quiet voice, "I'm just glad you're all right."

Did he really mean that? I looked over, but he kept his eyes on the road.

This man driving me home, with my picture on his desk, calling the police in case I was in trouble, he didn't match up to the man I'd lived with the past eight years. The one who never spoke to me, who never seemed to care whether I lived or died. This just wasn't the same guy. I couldn't figure it out, couldn't think straight anymore.

I closed my eyes again and drifted off.

"Christian. We're home." He tugged on my arm, pulling me out of the car.

I stumbled into the house and up the stairs, leaning heavily on the railing to drag myself up. Dad was there, one hand on my back steadying me as I climbed. I went into my bathroom and scrubbed my hands, watching the water in the sink turn red, swirling into a vortex as it went down the drain. Then I collapsed onto my bed.

* * *

I woke up drenched in sweat. Someone had covered me with two tons of blankets. With every heartbeat, a stabbing pain pulsed through my arm, and I was thirsty beyond belief. I checked the time: almost eight o'clock. I'd slept over seven hours.

A few bottles of water and a two-liter of soda sat on my nightstand, along with a bottle of extra-strength acetaminophen, ibuprofen, and a green plastic container of Percocet prescribed to Richard Morris, plus the extra dressing. My dad must've left them here before he went back to work.

I threw the blankets off and swung my legs over the side of the bed, sitting up. I rubbed my rib cage. "Ouch." With a click of the safety seal, I opened a bottle of water and drained it. Ibuprofen seemed like my best option; I picked up the bottle and checked the label. I avoided taking anything stronger if I didn't need it. Plus, I'd had a bad experience with prescription painkillers not too long ago. I didn't want to go there again.

"The doctor said you can take up to four."

I whipped my head around. My dad sat by the door in a stiff, high-backed chair carried up from the dining room table.

CHAPTER EIGHTEEN

CHRISTIAN VS. WEST HILLS MEMORIAL GARDENS

"WHAT ARE YOU DOING HERE?" I asked, popping the pills into my mouth and washing them down with another water bottle. My pants were stiff from the dried blood, and the left sleeve of my shirt dangled from my shoulder, covered in more blood. I looked like the lone survivor of a zombie apocalypse. I stood, holding my left arm against my side, and went into the closet. With some awkward one-handed maneuvering, I removed the blood-stained clothes and stuffed them in the garbage then pulled on sweats and a T-shirt.

When I came out, he was still there.

"I want to talk," he said.

Talk? After eight years of nothing, this was the second time in one week that my father approached me wanting to talk.

I didn't have the energy for this, not at the moment. I'd just had a bullet rip through my arm and had almost singlehandedly sent two girls to their graves. My stress capacity for one day had been maxed out.

I sat down on the bed. "I'm really tired," I told him.

"I know. But I want to say this before it's too late."

"Too late for what?" *Too late* had left the station a long time ago.

He ran a hand through his hair and then over his face. "When your mother died, I thought I'd lost the best part of my life. That there was nothing left for me."

Nothing. There was that word again. The one he'd used so many times to describe his only son. The one that choked me, that burned into my soul, branding me as worthless. How did he think this talk would help?

He leaned forward in the chair, elbows on his knees and eyes staring at the floor. "I was afraid. Afraid that if I let myself love again—love you—I'd lose you too. And I couldn't bear the thought."

I shook my head. I saw where this was headed. To some sort of wacked-out apology. Did he really expect me to accept such a lame excuse—he loved me so much, the only way he could live without fear of losing me was to hate me? Didn't he see how that had backfired? He'd lost me anyway.

He went on without looking up. "I distanced myself from you."

Understatement of the year.

"By the time I realized how much it hurt you, how wrong I'd been, I didn't know how to come back. When I came home Friday and you were gone—it was like when your mother died all over again." He finished in a whisper.

I had waited years for this moment, for validation of all I'd suffered because of him. But it had come too late. The damage was done. I would have given anything to hear this two weeks ago, when I was hovering near death on my bathroom floor, so desperate to make him care. But now I realized that all the words in the world couldn't give me back what I'd lost during my life alone. Nothing could make it right. I didn't want to hear any more.

I turned my back on him and slowly peeled the tape off my arm. The white gauze was wet and stiff. At least it was my blood and not Jenny's. I couldn't close my eyes without seeing her empty face staring up from a pool of red. And who knew what horrors Scarlett had had to endure. Maybe Detective Parker could find out something about her, but in my heart, I knew Scarlett was gone. I wanted to scream.

But not in front of my dad. He seemed to be waiting for me to say something. An answer to his confession.

"Okay." I was careful not to imply that I was okay, or our family was okay, or his messed-up parenting method was okay. Just an *I heard what you said* okay.

The hole in my arm still oozed. Maybe someday it would be cool to have a scar where a bullet went through me. It would mess up my tennis game for a while. I tried to wrap fresh cloth around it with one hand, but the gauze kept slipping.

My dad came over and took the bandage from me. He looped it around the wound. "If you still want to leave, I'll understand. And I'll help you however I can. But it would be nice if you would stay." His voice cracked as he finished speaking. He lifted his eyes from the bandage and looked straight into mine.

It seemed like he meant it. Like he was honestly reaching out and that it cost him a lot.

"Thanks," I said, lying down on the bed. The sweat on my body chilled me as it evaporated away. I pulled on one of the blankets.

He headed for the door then stopped and turned. "I know you won't believe me, but I do love—"

"Don't say it." I sat up. "Just don't. I'd rather not know." If he said those words, it would make both our lives a lie.

"I'll have Gloria bring up some food." He left, closing the door behind him.

I slammed my head back onto my pillows. It hurt.

If I had to choose between a father who loved me but treated me like garbage and one who simply didn't care enough to be bothered, I wanted the second. The pain of all those wasted years would be unbearable if I knew that the whole time he had secretly loved me.

Did he think he could rewind time with just a few words? Words that sounded more like an excuse than an actual apology? But that was probably the closest he would ever come. *I'm sorry* just wasn't part of his vocabulary.

Gloria came in carrying a cardboard takeout carton from my favorite Mexican place. She was dressed up in nice pants and a red sweater. She didn't usually wear her expensive jewelry this late into the evening. "Hey there. You feeling okay?"

"Yeah, just swell."

"I'm so glad." She set the carton on my bed. "Richard's been worried sick."

"Thanks for the food, Gloria."

She gave me a smile. "Do you need anything else?" she asked, checking her watch.

"No."

"Are you sure? Because I can stay if you need something." She seemed a little too eager.

"Stay?"

She fiddled with her wedding ring—a diamond the size of an almond—twisting it around her finger. "Monday's my Bunco night. Richard wouldn't let me go until you woke up."

Of course. How could I forget Gloria's Monday-night Bunco? "I'm fine. You should go." She patted my leg then left. Seconds later, I heard the garage open and close.

I ate the whole meal—steak burrito smothered in spicy cheese sauce. This late in the evening, it probably wasn't the best idea, but I was famished.

And still thirsty. I opened the two-liter of soda and started on that. The influx of food and sugary, caffeinated soft drink—combined with the mega-dose of ibuprofen—boosted my waning energy. I paced the room. I couldn't get Jenny's last pleading look out of my mind. Or Scarlett. Or the things my dad had just told me.

I wanted to go downstairs to watch TV and clear my head, to numb the pain that I couldn't palliate by simply swallowing a handful of tablets. But I didn't know if my dad would be there or if he'd retired to his bedroom like usual.

I looked out my window, east across the lights of Portland. Mount Hood was invisible in the dark. It always reminded me of my mother and how much she loved the cabin. Since my dad never went there after her death, it held only good memories for me.

The rain had stopped, and stars perforated the sky. To the north stretched the many miles of Forest Park and Mom's cemetery. She should be the one here, changing my bandage and bringing me food. I closed my eyes and tried to see her face. She was too far away. But I could still talk to her. I grabbed a coat from my closet and dug through my stuff until I found a flashlight then crept downstairs.

The house was quiet, so I assumed my dad had gone to his room. I took two steps toward the garage before remembering I'd left my car at Wyden's clinic. Footsteps in the hallway made me turn just as my dad rounded the corner. His face was drawn tight.

"Where are you going?"

He thought I was leaving him. I saw it in his eyes. "I can't sleep."

Dad pointed at my coat. "Are you cold?" Interpretation: You didn't answer my question.

"I wanted to go to the cemetery, but I think my car is still downtown."

His face relaxed. "They slashed your tires. I had it towed. Should be ready first thing in the morning."

I nodded. I guess Connor and Deepthroat didn't want another crazy ride through Portland.

He held up a hand. "Wait a minute." He turned and walked down the hall.

I couldn't get used to my father approaching me. Talking to me. Asking me to wait. Looking me in the eye. The handful of times we had spoken, we sort of talked to each other's shoulders or the floor. We'd gone for so long without eye contact, I struggled with it now.

He returned and tossed me his keys. "You can take my car."

"Are you sure?" I never expected an offer like that.

"Yes." I think he attempted some sort of smile, but it didn't last long enough for positive identification.

"Thanks." I felt like I needed to reboot my brain to make sense of this new, updated version of my dad. Father 2.0.

When I turned his car on, the radio was set to some intellectual AM station like National Public Radio. I popped open the center console to see if he had any kind of MP3 player plugged in. What I found was his gun. Or another gun. I couldn't be sure if it was the same one he'd had the other night when Scarlett had screamed. It seemed smaller to me. Over the years, he had put some nasty people behind bars, and I assumed he must get occasional threats. Carrying a gun made sense.

I snapped the console closed and settled for a satellite radio station to enjoy the smooth, powerful ride to West Hills Memorial Gardens.

The Forest Park trees bordering the cemetery gave the place a feeling of being on the edge of the wilderness. Most people didn't like cemeteries at night—they found them creepy. I loved it. So peaceful and quiet. My feet squelched as I walked slowly across the soggy lawn to Mom's grave near the cedar tree.

Last time I'd come here, I'd had Scarlett with me, kissing her while she stood on my mother's headstone. I wanted to feel her hand resting in the crook of my arm, her soft touch on my face.

Of course, that would never happen. Whatever Dr. Wyden and Simon were doing, they were down one minion with Connor out of the picture. They would move quickly to finish what they'd started, before the police could track them down.

I brushed some golden leaves off my mother's grave, offerings from the trees planted randomly amongst the dead. "I don't know what to do, Mom," I said out loud. "I think Dad wants me to forgive him. But I'm not sure if I can. Some things are unforgivable."

In my mind, I tallied the millions of times I'd really needed a father but he hadn't been there for me. Until today.

Wasn't this the moment I'd been waiting for? He'd said he cared, that he wanted me to stay. What if this was my only chance to bridge the gap? I'd messed up a lot in the past. I didn't want to blow it again. If I shut my dad out right when he wanted back in, how did that make me different from him? I'd vowed never to turn out like him.

If I really wanted to turn around, to fix my life like Jay wanted me to, I had to forgive my dad.

It was an act of faith. I had no guarantee he wouldn't abandon me again. *What if next week he decides I'm not worth the trouble?* Would I go back to *nothing?* Letting him into my life was a huge risk. I didn't think I could handle it if he turned on me again. On the other hand, what if he really did love me? I would never know unless I gave him a chance.

Nothing could change the past, but maybe this could be a fresh start. Not erasing all those years but moving forward from this point, going in a new direction. A different direction.

If I kept my eyes facing forward, things might still turn out okay.

At least for us. I didn't think I'd ever recover from my guilt about Scarlett and Jenny.

I gazed up at the stars and spoke to my mom again. "If you see my friend Scarlett, take care of her for me. And tell her I miss her more than . . ." I tried to think of what Scarlett would say, one of her crazy British sayings. I came up blank. "Just tell her, 'Crikey O'Reilly.'" That pretty much summed up everything.

I started back to the car, but I couldn't face going home yet. I wandered through the cemetery under the clear sky. A night like this was rare this time of year. I zipped my jacket.

I meandered through the gravestones, ending up close to the mortuary. Lights shone from the windows in the rear. There must have been a recent death. Maybe they were working on Jenny. Of course, she could've been at one of dozens of funeral homes in the area.

A couple of cars were parked in the rear driveway, next to the hearse. A morbid image of Jenny being loaded into it made me shudder. I doubted Scarlett would get that much dignity. She would simply vanish, and few would feel the loss. Some friends from her school and maybe her mom, if she cared enough to notice. And me.

I sat down on a cold granite bench in the mortuary gardens and hung my head, wishing again that the lava would swallow me up. I should head back and take my misery away from this peaceful place.

I stood to leave, but my eyes finally focused on what I'd been staring at. One of the cars in the mortuary carport was a black Tahoe. My breath caught, and the cold air chilled my lungs. I crept closer to check the bumper. *Someone in Oregon Loves Me.*

They were here.

CHAPTER NINETEEN

CHRISTIAN VS. THE CURE

I SMACKED MY PALM ON my forehead. How had I missed this? It made perfect sense. The mortuary had everything they needed. A perfect location for them to perform their sickening experiments. This had to be where they'd locked Scarlett until she'd escaped through the window and wandered the entire night, only to end up a few hundred yards away. Then, when I'd stopped here on my way out of town, she'd climbed into my car and changed my life.

She could be in there.

I ran forward then stopped. *Don't be stupid this time, Morris.*

They'd always been one step ahead of me, outsmarting me at every turn. I ducked behind the Tahoe to call for help. I patted the pockets of my sweats and coat. Oh yeah. My cell phone sat on my bathroom counter, crusty with blood—still in the baggie from Parker.

Did I have time to go back to the house? If Scarlett was in there and still alive, every second counted. I couldn't spare half an hour for there and back. I hurried to the car, took Dad's gun from between the seats, and ran to the building. I really hoped I wouldn't have to use it, but I needed some backup, and this was all I had.

"Dad," I whispered, closing my eyes and concentrating on some invisible ESP link that I knew didn't exist. "I've never asked you for anything. But I'm asking now. When I don't come home, call for help."

Okay. *Think.* How to get inside. A mortuary would definitely have a security system—they wouldn't want anyone breaking in and body snatching. But they must not monitor it closely or else Scarlett wouldn't have gotten away so easily. She climbed out of a window above ground without setting off an alarm. Maybe the alarm was wired only to the main doors. This was an old building, and it was possible the security system might not be up-to-date.

I peered around the side of the car, scanning the eaves for cameras. I found one centered above the garage, between the back door on one side and the loading bay on the other. I circled the structure, searching for a way in.

Scarlett said she'd landed on mulch, so I needed a window without bushes below. The funeral home was carefully landscaped. An attempt to make the families of the dead feel good about their choice of mortuary. Around the side, a room jutted from the building, its paint a little cleaner than the rest. A new addition—and no azaleas under the window.

I pulled on it. Locked. Most likely, they'd found it open after Scarlett's escape and had remedied their oversight. I checked every window, tugging at the casings, but all were secure. Now what? I'd have to try the doors and risk setting off an alarm. Front, back, or loading bay? All the doors were in full view of a camera.

Still, sneaking in where I might be caught on video seemed less risky than smashing a window. The back entrances were closest to the carport; maybe they left them unlocked after going in. I'd try the smaller door, hoping to get in farther away from the main area of use.

I sidled up to the door, completely exposed by the floodlights in the carport's ceiling. I steadied the gun in my hand and reached out, quietly grasping the smooth, cold doorknob. With a deep breath, I gave it a slow turn. It was open.

I cracked the large steel door enough to discover that it led to a narrow hallway. The lights were off at this end, but a glow emanated from around the corner. I slipped inside and noiselessly closed the metal door behind me.

To the right was solid wall. To the left, the corridor carried on straight ahead and a smaller hallway branched off. I stuck my head around the corner. Lights and voices came from a room down that way. I went straight, crossing the intersection in two steps, careful not to make a sound on the hard linoleum floor.

I opened the first door I came to. It was a viewing room. A coffin sat on a wheeled metal cart in the front. I had to check. Bracing myself for the worst, I lifted the lid. It was empty. Of course they wouldn't store a murdered body in a public room. I let out a breath.

I crossed the hall and entered another room. An office. I clicked on my flashlight and made a quick scan of the desk. A stack of business cards propped upright in a brass holder sat on the corner. I picked one up and read it: *Gary Wyden; Forest Park Mortuary*. Accompanying this information was a picture of Deepthroat. He was Dr. Anne Wyden's brother, the resemblance obvious to me now. In the photo, he wore a dark suit and smiled, warm and friendly, looking like the perfect man to take care of all of your funeral needs.

I stuffed the card in my pocket. If I ever got out of here alive, I'd show it to Detective Parker. Although, he'd probably already figured it out. Seemed everyone knew more about this than I did.

The base of a cordless phone sat next to the cards, but I couldn't find the handset anywhere.

I slipped out and tried the next door. It opened into a large room. I swept the flashlight across the darkness and saw rows of pews, like at church. The funeral chapel. Following the hall took me around a corner and through the front lobby, where a cloth sofa and plush chairs were arranged around end tables, like a living room. Mottled-brown carpeting covered the floor at this end of the building, making the chapel and lobby homier and less industrial looking. I turned down the hall on the opposite side of the one I'd just checked.

I found another viewing room, this one without a casket. About twenty feet farther down, lights shone from under two doors, along with the quiet murmur of voices. I'd made a complete U around the corridors of the mortuary. At the end of the hall were an elevator and the loading-bay doors that opened into the driveway across from where I'd come in.

With my back against the wall and the gun in my hand, I listened outside the first door. Nothing. The voices were coming from the next room a few yards down the hall.

Either they'd left the light on, or I'd step into this room and come face-to-face with one of the kidnappers. If it was Simon, I'd shoot him on the spot. I thought my chances were about fifty-fifty that I'd be dead in the next five minutes.

I turned the knob quickly and slipped inside. On a hard, stainless-steel autopsy table lay Scarlett, her pink hair matted and stuck to her face. Her eyes closed. I reached her in one stride, brushing the stray strands from her forehead. Her skin was warm, and her chest rose and fell with slow, rhythmic breathing. Alive.

An IV pumped fluid into her arm through a long plastic tube stuck in at her elbow. I stashed the gun in my coat pocket and patted her cheek.

"Scarlett," I whispered. She didn't move. I checked the label on the IV bag. *Diprivan.* What did that do? Knock her out, or keep her alive? It didn't matter. She had a better chance of survival away from this place, with or without the drugs.

I tugged the tape off the IV and pulled the needle out. A thin line of red leaked onto her pasty white skin.

"Scarlett." I slapped her cheek again, harder. I couldn't waste any more time in here. "Come on." I lifted her from the table, groaning as the effort shot pain through my arm. Her feet bumped the autopsy table and the steel clanked.

She let out a soft moan. "Christian?"

At least, that's what it sounded like. She was barely audible.

"Yes." I would have put her fingers on my face, but my hands were full. "It's me."

The smallest smile touched her lips. I turned around to open the door. I'd take her out the way I came in, around through the lobby and out the back door—avoiding the rooms with lights and voices.

The door opened for me.

Simon Lawrence stood there, his face a mirror of my own surprise. Then he grinned. "Finally figured it out, did you?"

"Out of my way, berk!" I kicked him as hard as I could in the gut. He fell backward, and I bolted for the front entrance. No reason to avoid setting off alarms now. I heard Deepthroat—Gary—call after me. I didn't stop. A gun fired, and a bullet smacked into the wall as I turned the corner. No wonder Connor had always carried the gun. Gary was a crap shot.

"Don't shoot. You'll kill her. We need her alive." I recognized Dr. Wyden's smooth voice.

I struck at the metal bar to open the door with my foot, but it was bolted shut. I ran down the other hall with Scarlett bouncing in my arms. The lights flicked on, and Simon and Dr. Wyden stood there, blocking my way out, Simon with a gun in his hand. I stopped.

I thought about diving into the chapel, but that was a dead end. This whole place was a dead end.

Something cracked against my skull, and I dropped to the floor, spilling Scarlett out onto the cold, hard ground.

* * *

Darkness. And cold. Freezing cold. My head hung backward, limp on my neck. I tried to lift it, but it was so heavy. When I finally unglued my eyelids, I found myself staring at white ceiling tiles crisscrossed with thin metal lines and a fluorescent light strip. I managed to lift my head. Duct tape bound my arms and legs to an old industrial-style office chair with a steel frame and a mint-green vinyl seat.

Two bodies were laid out on gurneys behind me, their identities covered with green sheets. A storage room. For dead people. Did they die of natural causes, or were they victims of Dr. Wyden's work? Was one of them Scarlett? How long had I been out?

"No!" I yelled. I'd had her in my hands, only to lose her again.

The door opened, and Dr. Wyden came in. She didn't look quite as put together as she did in her glamour shot on the Retinal Implant flier. Strands of hair fell from the knot piled on top of her head, and her stylish glasses had slipped to the bottom of her nose and sat at an awkward angle. Simon trotted along behind her. Even with her flat shoes, she was a few inches taller than her husband.

"Christian Morris." She smiled at me and lifted her glasses so they rested on the top of her head. "Nice to see you again," she said in her deep, soothing voice. Her white lab coat and friendly smile made her look like your average family eye doctor.

"Where's Scarlett?" I asked.

"Upstairs. She's fine." She waved a hand as if kidnapping Scarlett and subjecting her to some twisted medical procedure was just another day at the office.

At least they hadn't killed her yet. "What are you going to do with her?"

Dr. Wyden's eyes sparked with excitement, and she licked her lips. "I'm testing something on her. Something that will change the lives of sightless people around the world."

"You mean change the life of your daughter." She didn't fool me. That's what this had been about all along.

A steeliness entered her voice. "So you did learn something when you destroyed my office and ruined my clinic." She came closer, standing right in front of me so I had to crane my neck to see her face. I didn't appreciate the nostril view. Simon stood by the door, stoic, with a gun in his hand.

She squatted down to eye level. "But you're wrong. Can't you see? This goes far beyond my Mags." Her eyes glowed. "Thanks to Scarlett's genius friend, I've developed a new device. Simon's been keeping an eye on Katie for a while, as the IT technician at Shepherd Hill. After Katie created her auditory amplifier, it didn't take much for Simon to convince her to turn her talents on an innovation to help her best friend." She tossed Simon an adoring look.

"With a little input from Katie"—Dr. Wyden stood up and started pacing the room as if all this was too awesome to tell standing still— "I've developed a nanocamera that connects directly to the optic nerve, bypassing the retina altogether. It inserts into the pupil, allowing color vision in a resolution close to normal. Unfortunately, the optic nerve is very sensitive. Too little stimulation and nothing happens. Too much and, well, poof." She lifted a hand and made an exploding gesture by her head. "The brain is fried. It's a very delicate balance."

How many people had she tested this on? Had it ever worked? Scarlett was never going to survive. Not that Jenny was my standard of optic knowledge, but based on what she'd said, this could never happen. The nerves to the brain could not be repaired.

"Can't you test it on animals? Dogs or something?" I asked. Her Frankenstein methods didn't seem quite in line with current FDA standards.

She sighed heavily and shook her head. "We tried. But when we repeated the experiment on a human, the data didn't transfer. We had to start over." She seemed genuinely disappointed.

"You're psychotic." All this so her daughter could see? Did Maggie know her mother was killing people to restore her vision?

"Christian, try to understand. This project will bring sight to millions." She swept her hands wide to encompass the whole world, and her eyes burned with the promise of victory. "Picture it. The end of blindness. A scourge that has plagued the earth since the beginning of time. Unfortunately, miracles through science require some sacrifices. Scarlett is proud to help in such a generous cause, don't you think?"

This was insane. Wyden really believed that she was some kind of crusader. That her perverted work on innocent people was justified. She walked back to Simon, stood beside him, and smiled as if there was no way I could argue against such a noble undertaking.

"Makes sense," I said, grasping at straws to buy time. "Scarlett probably is happy to help. Why not just let me go?"

Simon shook his head. "So you can run to your police friend? I think not. Unfortunately, when you hooked up with Scarlett, you sort of sealed your fate. Can't have you blathering about our work to everyone now, can we?"

I stared at him. "Is that why you want me? So I won't tell someone that you're murderers?"

"Hey," Simon said. I didn't think he knew much about guns. He held it awkwardly in his hand, and as he spoke, he swung it carelessly in all directions. He must have noticed me watching it because he let his arm fall to his side, aiming the gun at the floor. "We didn't *murder* anyone. Any kind of medical procedure involves risks."

"What about Jenny? And the waitress?" I asked.

He waved the gun in dismissal, forgetting his previous attempt to keep it still. "*That*," he said with emphasis, "was Connor."

Dr. Wyden jumped to her husband's defense. "Connor was crazy. We hired him to help us with Scarlett's abduc—" She glanced at the floor. "Transportation. He got a little carried away."

Sure. If you call shooting two innocent people *a little carried away.* Not to mention attacking Scarlett in the Lloyd Center and chasing me from school in the middle of class.

"He was out of control," Simon said. "I'm not sorry he's gone."

Dr. Wyden shook her head and spoke to Simon like I wasn't in the room. "We could have used him in a trial."

Simon nodded, and they considered each other for a moment. I watched some kind of unspoken conversation pass between them, then they both turned and looked at me.

"Good idea," he said.

My skin prickled. Now they wanted to operate on me? "But I'm not blind."

She laughed. "We can fix that so easily." She left the room.

Simon turned back to me. "Thanks again for taking such good care of Scarlett. I really think she's going to be the breakthrough." Then he shrugged. "But I thought that about the last one too." He followed Wyden out the door, his face thoughtful.

So Scarlett's dreams would all come true. If we were talking about most people's dreams, that would be a happy thought. But it wasn't with her dreams. For Scarlett and me, it meant death. Scarlett on the operating table. And me, here in this room. Regardless of Wyden's schemes to experiment on me, I had Scarlett's dream to tell me I would avoid the surgical knife. The two dead bodies behind me and Simon's gun were enough to convince me that this was the scene of my death. Soon, I would be the one lying on the floor with my blood staining the tiles.

I strained my hands against the silver tape, twisting and pulling. They didn't give. *Dad, call for help*! I pleaded in my mind. He'd probably gone to bed. Gloria wouldn't be home from Bunco for hours.

I had left my father—twice in the last few days—with the intention of never seeing him again. But as I sat taped to a chair with permanent separation in my very near future, I knew I'd been lying to myself all along.

I'd always wanted to see him again. I'd just wanted him to suffer like I'd suffered. Then maybe he'd realize he cared about me. I craved his attention now as much as I did the day I swallowed the bottle of pills. Earlier this evening, I'd thought he was finally ready to try. But I hadn't let him, and now it was too late. I groaned, remembering what I'd said to him in his office. I wished I could take back my words. Tell him how I felt.

If he really did want a second chance, my death would torment him the rest of his life. What would he do? Turn on Gloria? That wasn't what I wanted, but I grinned anyway then shook my head. I could live with Gloria, if I got a chance to live.

I had to change fate. Undo Scarlett's dream. I was in control of my own destiny, and it would not end here. Neither would Scarlett's. I worked on the duct tape again, twisting and pulling to loosen the bonds.

I lowered my head to bite the tape, but I couldn't reach it. I scanned the room for anything I could use. A cabinet with a big vat of something next to it stood against one wall. The vat plus the drain in the middle of the floor and the strong smell of formaldehyde gave me a pretty good idea of what this room was used for.

I scooted toward the cabinet, using the weight of my body to lurch the chair across the floor. I tried to be stealthy, but the clanging of the metal legs sounded like a stampede of linebackers wearing steel cleats. I finally got close enough to open the cupboard door with my teeth. I stared, momentarily transfixed by the bottles and boxes of embalming supplies. Lots of hexaphene—whatever that was—a metal jar of *Leakproof Skin*, a tub of mortician's wax, and an ominous carton with a photo of a spiky-looking mouth guard labeled *Natural Expression Mouth Former*. Yuck. There was one potential profession I could cross off my list.

On the opposite side of the room was a small chest of drawers made of steel. I crossed the room again, sweating with the exertion, even in the freezing temperature. I wore my coat, and a weight in the pocket gave me hope that my dad's gun was still there.

They had to hear me clattering around, but maybe they didn't care. I opened the first drawer. Inside, a tray full of surgical instruments rattled.

One was a scalpel with a long, thin blade. Again, with my mouth, and bending at a very uncomfortable angle, I got it out of the drawer, seriously hoping it had been sterilized since its last use. But I wondered, because if they were dead, what was the point of preventing cross-contamination?

I transferred the blade to my hand, twisting it in my fingers until I had it aimed backward at the tape on my wrist. I sawed through, slicing open a few spots on my skin in the attempt. When I got one hand free, it took only seconds to finish the job. I pulled the tape off my wrists—along with a layer of skin—and then undid my feet.

I had to check the bodies. Wyden could have lied about Scarlett's still being alive. I lifted the sheets off their faces, one at a time. The first one was an elderly Asian man. He looked normal—for a dead guy. No dangling eyes or blood seeping out his ears from a fried brain.

My mind flashed back to my mother's funeral. Her pale face blank and lifeless. My dad had lifted me up in his arms so I could see into the casket. I'd tried to tell him it wasn't her. It didn't look like her. I buried my head in his shoulder and cried while he stroked my back, one of his silent tears falling on my face. The next day, we were strangers.

I reached out to feel the dead man's skin. It was like touching a refrigerated grapefruit.

I slipped the sheet off the second body and jumped back. It was a woman with black holes where her eyes should have been. She looked maybe Gloria's age, and other than the vacant sockets, she seemed undamaged. If I didn't hurry, that would be Scarlett.

The door to the cold room was thick and solid. I pulled it open and stepped into the stairwell. To my left, stairs led up to another door, and straight ahead, there was an elevator. I figured they must use the elevator for transporting bodies up and down from the cold room. I grabbed my dad's gun out of my pocket. I'd never fired one before and was probably no better than Simon. With my luck, I'd shoot my eye out. At least then Wyden wouldn't be able to practice on me.

I crept up the stairs and cracked the door. The hallway was deserted, as was Scarlett's room—her gurney was gone. They must have started the operation next door. Katie and possibly Maggie might also be in there. In Scarlett's dream, Katie was watching, helping. Probably like Scarlett, she didn't have a choice.

I paused with my hand on the knob. What now? Open the door and shoot? I didn't want to kill anyone—except maybe Simon. But how else could I get Scarlett out alive?

I took several quick breaths and gave the handle a silent turn, opening it to a tiny slit and peeking in. Dr. Wyden was bent over some tiny equipment, jabbing at something with a pair of tweezers. Gary stood poised over Scarlett, ready with a needle to hook her up to the IV again. A girl Scarlett's age sat on a folding chair in the corner. She had a frizz of red hair and more freckles than skin. I couldn't see Simon, but I knew he was in there, out of sight, blocked by the door.

When I pulled the door open, Simon was the first to respond. He reached for his gun on the counter behind him. I aimed at his torso, hoping to incapacitate rather than kill. I squeezed the trigger and the explosion cracked the air, my ears ringing with the blast. He slammed back into the counter and fell to the floor.

Gary turned on me, throwing punches. "Run, Scarlett," I yelled while trying to block him.

"Katie!" Scarlett screamed.

Katie jumped from her chair and started working on the tape that secured Scarlett's hands and legs, slicing through it with a scalpel. I threw myself on Gary, shoving him into the medical equipment that lined the walls. He lost his balance and fell backward.

Katie grabbed Scarlett's hand, and they ran for the door. Wyden cut them off, pointing Simon's gun at Katie. In the midst of all the commotion, I registered Wyden's instincts. She lived with a blind daughter and knew that pointing the gun at Scarlett would do nothing. Katie, however, came to a halt.

Wyden slipped her gun into her lab-coat pocket. She grabbed Katie and Scarlett and towed them from the room. Scarlett struggled against her, trying to jerk her arm out of Wyden's grip. Katie withered. Maybe she'd been with them too long and had already given up.

Gary scrambled off the floor, and I turned my gun on him. "Stop, or I'll shoot."

He flashed a wild grin. I pulled the trigger. My shot grazed his side but didn't stop him. He came at me again, one fist slamming into my face and the other into my gut. I doubled over, and he cracked something heavy across my back.

I staggered to the side, fighting to aim my gun at him. I fired again, and Gary spun around, hitting the floor face first. He moaned but didn't get up.

"Christian!" Scarlett called.

I ran into the hallway, hunched over from the blow to my back. Wyden was dragging the girls toward the back door and the carport.

"Stop, Wyden. Stop right there."

She released the terrified girls. I didn't dare shoot with Scarlett and Katie so close. My hesitation gave Wyden time to point her gun at me.

"Run away, Scarlett," I said. "When you find someone, tell them to take you to my dad." He liked Scarlett, and he'd look out for her—in case Wyden pulled the trigger first.

The girls turned and went down the hall toward the front of the building, Katie tugging Scarlett along.

"What do we do now?" Dr. Wyden asked in her cotton-fluff voice.

"You drop your gun, and I call the police. Now where's that roll of duct tape?"

She chuckled, but her eyes were bricks. "I don't think so. You got Scarlett. There's no reason to kill me." She bolted through the door.

I threw a quick glance behind me. Scarlett and Katie were gone. I followed Wyden through the door. She climbed into a car and threw it in reverse, backing out like a maniac and then grinding her engine when she slammed it into gear.

She sped down the driveway. Something smacked across my head, and the world went black.

* * *

Not again, I thought in the haze of waking. I expected to open my eyes and find the ceiling tiles, feel the chill of the refrigerated room in my bones. I didn't. I opened my eyes and found myself face-to-face with Detective Scott Parker.

"He called for help," I said, my voice shaky.

Parker nodded. "He did."

I was sitting in one of the plush chairs in the lobby, a paramedic holding a cold compress to my head. Red and blue flashes of light circled the room from the ambulances and police cars outside.

"She got away," I said.

"Who?" Parker asked.

"Dr. Wyden. She got away."

The detective shook his head. "We got her."

"Good." I grinned at him. "You know, you really need to work on your timing. Always five minutes too late." I leaned my head back against the wall and breathed deeply. My shoulders ached, and a steamroller slowly crushed my head. I looked at the paramedic. "Where's that morphine I had last time?"

It wasn't the same guy, and he didn't smile.

"I got this," I said, taking the cold compress. He walked away. My gaze fell on Parker, meeting his eyes. "I shot two people."

"I know. Gary Wyden is dead."

So there it was. I killed a man. I thought I should feel worse about it than I did. Maybe it would hit me later, when the vision of Scarlett being prepped for death surgery cleared from my mind. At the moment I'd pulled the trigger, I'd known it was the right thing to do.

"Can you tell me what happened?"

It was Parker's favorite question.

I recounted the events, starting with my visit to the grave. Parker was impressed that I'd figured it all out while his men were still scouring the clinic. I told him I hadn't figured out anything. I'd been doing what I do best—wandering aimlessly—when I happened to notice the Tahoe in the driveway. "Providence," I said. He asked about Dr. Wyden's experiments. And that's when it hit me that something was missing.

"Where's Scarlett?"

Detective Parker shook his head. "Sorry, slugger. We didn't find Scarlett. Or Simon Lawrence."

CHAPTER TWENTY

CHRISTIAN VS. THE SECOND HALF

"No."

"I'm sorry." Parker looked tired. It was the middle of the night, and he was still out chasing murderers and telling kids the people they loved were dead. Well, gone, and most likely dead.

I slowly paced the carpeted floor of the entrance, limping. "How can that be? I shot him. I watched Scarlett and Katie get away." Maybe I didn't injure him as much as I'd thought. *Note to self: Aim to kill.* "What about Katie?"

"He got a few rounds into her. They already took her to the hospital." Parker shook his head. "It doesn't look good."

Why would Simon take Scarlett and leave Katie? Katie was the genius. The chosen one to help bring sight to the world. Did Simon really have a thing for Scarlett? Maybe he had once. Apart from his wife for months at a time, a man can get desperate. I'd assumed they'd chosen Scarlett instead of a local blind person because of her dreams, to keep her from telling. Now everyone knew his crimes anyway. It didn't make sense.

"I shot him in the operating room," I said again. "I saw him go down. And you're telling me he got away with Scarlett?" She would have fought back, right? Now that she knew who Simon really was.

"We've searched the entire place, top to bottom. I've got men combing the grounds. She's not here." Parker laid his hand on my shoulder.

I jerked away. "No. He didn't get her." I pointed a finger at him and yelled. "He did *not* get her again!" I threw my cold compress to the ground. It smacked with a hollow thunk against a cupboard at the base of a large end table.

Remembering the bathroom at Shari's and the garbage can at Mount Hood, I opened it. Empty.

"She's here," I said. "I know it."

"We've looked everywhere."

"No. This is what she does. She hides. And she doesn't come out. No matter what." She was here. "Scarlett," I called.

I walked the halls with Detective Parker at my side. I think he thought I might collapse any minute, and he was probably right. Every part of me ached. "Scarlett!"

I checked every room, opening cupboards and looking under desks and rows of pews.

"She's gone," he said again.

I turned on him and roared, "She's not gone!"

He stepped back, and his eyebrows rose.

"Sorry." It wasn't his fault; it was mine. If I had done anything right, Scarlett would be in my arms right now. "This is what she does. I'll find her. She'll only come out for me." I hoped.

I checked the operating room. Gary's body was gone, but blood covered the floor. "Scarlett! You can come out now. I promise it's safe."

Nothing.

I thundered down the stairs, back to the refrigerated embalming room. She wasn't there either.

I rounded the corner and headed toward the doors where I'd first entered the building however many hours ago that was. I searched Gary's office, pulling books and files from every possible hiding place, my desperation rising with every empty closet. She wasn't there.

I went into the viewing room. "Scarlett! If you don't come out right this second—" I didn't finish the threat.

The lid to the coffin rose a few inches.

I ran over and flung it open.

She was there.

Somehow, she'd climbed the metal scaffolding of the rolling table, scrambled into the casket, and worked her way under the lining. If you glanced in quickly, you wouldn't see anyone there, just an empty coffin.

I ripped the silky white padding all the way off and lifted her out, ignoring the searing pain in my body. "You are in so much trouble." I hugged her as hard as I could. "We had a deal."

"'Bout time," she said. She held on tight, her arms around my neck and her feet dangling a foot off the ground.

The paramedics came in after us, wanting to take Scarlett to the ambulance to be checked out. I wouldn't let go. Not again. She put her hand in the crook of my arm. I loved it there.

After another half hour of probing by the medical personnel—and questioning from Parker—I was pronounced banged up, but okay. Parker said we could go. Actually, what he said was, "You look like a cat in the blender. I'll take you home."

He confiscated my dad's gun for evidence and said he'd come by tomorrow to see how we were. He loaded us into the back of a police cruiser.

We were home in ten minutes. Lights shone from my dad's study, even though the green digital clock on Parker's dash said two a.m.

Parker walked us to the door.

"Thanks," I said to him. "I owe you my life. And Scarlett's."

"That's twice now." He grinned. "Let's not make it a third, all right, cowboy?"

"All right."

I opened the door and stepped inside. I'd never been so tired in my whole life. My head pounded, and my ribs burned. I'd been shot and beaten up and had some kind of medical prop broken across my back. All I wanted now was to go upstairs, take one of every pill on my nightstand, and sleep for at least twenty-four hours. And then—shower.

My dad stepped out of his study. His steely gray eyes locked on me. I looked away.

I whispered into Scarlett's ear, "He's waiting for me. You go up. I'll be there in a minute."

"Okay." She climbed the stairs and disappeared into her room.

I took a deep breath and then lifted my gaze to my father's. He'd always been so tall, taller than me by a good two inches. Tonight, his shoulders drooped, and he seemed old and tired. Worn out. Afraid. Probably how I looked too. He didn't speak, waiting for me to say the first words.

"Parker said you called."

He nodded. "When you didn't come home, I worried." His voice broke, and he pinched his lips together.

"Thanks. If he hadn't shown up . . ." I didn't need to finish. We both knew the ending.

"Are you all right?"

I could see the effort it cost him to keep his eyes on mine. He wanted to look away, relieve the tension.

I felt the same way—encumbered by guilt and shame for my cruel words. Those were hard things to face eye to eye. And he had so much more to face than I did. I shrugged with my good arm. "I didn't get shot, so that's good."

He huffed a feeble laugh then rubbed his eyes. "Son, I am so sorry."

I think I would have been okay if he had said anything besides *son*. But he didn't. He said it like he meant it, like he was proud to be my father, and I lost it. I broke down, my body shaking as I tried to get back in control. I was a kid again. A child. Not the guy who'd shot a man to save the girl he loved but the one who needed saving.

I lowered myself onto the stairs, sitting with my head in my hands, blinking hard. He came and sat beside me, putting his arm across my shoulders, squeezing, pulling me close. I let it all go—leaning my head in and crying like I hadn't cried since I'd watched my mother die.

"Dad," I said.

After a few minutes, he said, "It's late; you should get to bed. You look terrible."

"So I've been told." I stood up, climbing the stairs with my last reserves of energy. I flung the covers back and slid into bed, too tired to take any medication.

What would things be like tomorrow? It had been a long day, and we were both exhausted. Eight years couldn't be fixed in five minutes. I knew that. I figured we had some awkward months ahead of us, followed by more only slightly less awkward years. But that was okay. It would be worth it.

* * *

I woke up with the sun streaming through my window and my body on fire. And someone knocking softly on my door.

"Yeah?"

The door opened, revealing Scarlett. She looked like she'd just woken up too. Her pink hair formed a fuzzy tangle around her face, and she was wearing sweat pants and a Barry Manilow T-shirt that could have come only from Gloria.

"Can I come in?" She brandished her mischievous grin. "I don't want to muck up your boundaries."

Nice to know Scarlett was okay. "You can come in."

She sat on the edge of my bed. "I guess you're the hero now."

"I don't know. Maybe." I had managed to save her, but I would have felt a lot better if Jenny was still alive.

Scarlett lifted the hand of my nonbullet-hole arm and placed it on the side of her face. "Thanks," she said, her voice suddenly serious.

I pulled her close and kissed her. "Well, someone has to look out for you foreigners."

I tried to scoot up in the bed so I could sit, but the muscles in my arm didn't cooperate. A new selection of water bottles had appeared on my nightstand. I opened one and drank it, along with a small handful of Ibuprofen.

"I thought you'd come in and say good night," she said.

"I meant to, but I barely made it up the stairs. One extra step would've been my last." I should've gone in, but I was a mess and not quite ready to talk about it yet. "What happened?" I asked. "What happened after you left here with Simon?"

She shuddered. "Christian, I had no idea he was married to her. I can't believe I was so thick. I thought he was a nice guy. Just goes to show, you can't trust anyone."

"You can trust me."

"I know." She touched my face, her fingers soft and light, impossible to resist.

I managed to push myself up so I was sitting this time, leaning back against the headboard. She told me how Simon took her straight to the mortuary. Turned her over to Dr. Wyden without any hesitation. They had planned to do the surgery that night, but Katie said the nanocamera wasn't ready. She stalled but could put them off only for one day.

"I heard you trashed her clinic," Scarlett said, laughing.

"I don't know if that's what I'd say exactly. But I went to her office to find out why Connor and Gary kept following me even after you were gone. They tried to kill me at school that morning. At the clinic, the receptionist—Jenny, remember her?"

"The appointment girl?"

"Right. She helped me search Dr. Wyden's office. That's when I found a photograph of Dr. Wyden, Simon, and their daughter. I knew then you'd been taken. They found me at the clinic. Connor shot Jenny."

"He killed her?"

"Yes. For no reason. Another casualty of Wyden's freak-tastic plans."

"It's because she saw them. Simon told me if I hadn't had my dream, none of this would've happened." She was quiet for a moment then said, "It's over now. And Dr. Wyden is locked up. No one else will get hurt. Everything worked out fine."

"Fine? A girl is dead; Katie is in the hospital; I have a bullet hole through my arm and probably a concussion. Or two."

She wanted to feel the damage from Connor's gun. I pulled up my sleeve and found the bandage soaked. I hadn't changed it last night, and all the exertion had kept the blood flowing.

I undid the tape, pulling it off gingerly, then unwound the long strip of gauze, exposing a mass of dried blood and gunk. Was I supposed to have it checked today? I didn't have the energy to leave the house for anything.

I still wore the sweats I'd put on last night, and I stank of sweat, blood, and the chemicals from the embalming room.

"Scarlett, I need a shower." But right after I said it, I remembered I couldn't take a shower; the hole in my arm had to stay dry. "Well, a bath."

"Okay," She kissed my cheek and left for her own room.

I went into my bathroom and took off my shirt in front of the mirror. A bruise the size of a frying pan covered half my ribs. I had another bruise on my cheek, and when I turned around, a welt like someone had hit me with a baseball bat crossed my back. I filled the tub with hot water and lowered myself in, careful to keep the bullet wound dry.

I soaked for a long time with my eyes closed. Then I dressed and tried to bandage my arm. I couldn't do it one-handed. I thought of asking Scarlett for help, but I heard her shower running. I stepped into the hall and called over the railing, "Gloria?"

My dad's face appeared in the hall. "She went to the store."

He looked like a different man from the one last night. Tall again, and straight. He really had been worried. Panicked that his son would die. Why wasn't he at work? It was Tuesday morning. He worked seven days a week. He watched me with a knot in his brow, wondering, like me, if anything had really changed between us.

If he was trying this hard, I could too. "Uh, I need some help here, with my arm." I held up the roll of cotton gauze.

He tried to keep his face straight, but I caught the relief that smoothed his forehead. He jogged up the stairs, two at a time. "Sure."

I sat on the edge of my bed, and he knelt on the floor in front of me. He wound the bandage around more times than probably necessary before securing it with tape. "How are you feeling today?" His words came out stiff and forced. This was going to be a bumpy road.

"Okay." I took a deep breath before making my next attempt at bridging the gap. "I'm sorry for the things I said at your office yesterday." I wished I could tell him I didn't really mean them, but at the time, I totally did. "I just . . . I mean, I was . . . The thing is . . ."

"Stop." He kept his focus on the bandaging, even though he'd already finished. "Don't worry about it. You were right, and I deserved every word. It's my fault."

I never expected to hear words like that come from him—words that didn't choke and strangle but instead settled on me softly, peacefully. I think at last he understood all the torture he'd put me through. But if he wanted a son, and I wanted a father, I couldn't think like that anymore. I had to let it go.

"Okay, then," I said. "Let's just move on."

His whole body relaxed. "Yes. If you'll give me the chance."

I think I'd been around Scarlett too long. I couldn't resist the urge to get him back for his wisecracks the other night when he'd nearly shot me with his gun. I carefully edged my voice with humor and said, "Will you toss out all your bottles of wine?"

He looked me straight in the eye. "I already did."

I stared at him, stunned. I had no comeback for that.

A thin smile crossed his face, and he patted my knee, like a stranger pats the head of a wandering dog. I'd take it.

He left as Scarlett came in.

"What was that about?" Her pink hair fell around her face, still wet and shiny from the shower, and her diamond nose stud glittered in the morning sun streaming through the window. She sat beside me, resting her head on my shoulder.

"Scarlett, you called it. I think the second half is going to be okay."

ABOUT THE AUTHOR

JULIE DAINES WAS BORN IN Concord, Massachusetts, and was raised in Utah. She spent eighteen months living in London, where she studied and fell in love with English literature, sticky toffee pudding, and the mysterious guy who ran the kebab store around the corner.

She loves reading, writing, and watching movies—anything that transports her to another world. She picks Captain Wentworth over Mr. Darcy, firmly believes in second breakfast, and never leaves home without her *verveine*.

To learn more about Julie Daines or to contact her, visit her website at www.juliedaines.com.